IN THE HEART OF LOVE

Alison Ross's humdrum life is violently changed when kidnappers take her daughter, Susi, mistaking her for the granddaughter of business tycoon David Beresford, in whose offices Alison is employed. The kidnappers realise their mistake and Susi's life is in danger. Now Alison's peaceful existence in the Devon countryside becomes embroiled not only in horror, but also unexpected romance. But this is threatened by spiteful gossip concerning her innocent relationships with the two men who wish to marry her . . .

JUDY CHARD

IN THE HEART OF LOVE

Complete and Unabridged

LINFORD
Leicester

First published in Great Britain in 1978

First Linford Edition
published 2006

British Library CIP Data

Chard, Judy
In the heart of love.—Large print ed.—
Linford romance library
1. Kidnapping—Fiction
2. Devon (England)—Fiction
3. Love stories 4. Large type books
I. Title
823.9'14 [F]

ISBN 1–84617–563–1

Published by
F. A. Thorpe (Publishing)
Anstey, Leicestershire

Set by Words & Graphics Ltd.
Anstey, Leicestershire
Printed and bound in Great Britain by
T. J. International Ltd., Padstow, Cornwall

This book is printed on acid-free paper

1

The August sun beat relentlessly through the open windows of Beresford's offices.

Alison Ross glanced up from her typewriter, gazing at the fields, burnt crisp and brown by the long summer, at the wilting trees and hedges. A bluebottle buzzed, caught in a web at the window . . .

For a moment she thought of cool blue seas, sandy coves and wheeling gulls . . .

A voice broke into her reveries . . .

'There won't be any need for anyone to go to the Costa What's It for sun this year,' Brenda Pearse said from the neighbouring desk, 'honestly I wouldn't have believed it but I'm sick of the sight of sun . . . thank heavens it's Friday. Guy and I are off to the coast the whole weekend. Heaven . . . '

'Lucky old so and so,' someone else added, and then a voice asked, 'What you doing, Ali? Taking Susi on the beach?'

Alison withdrew her gaze from the fields and trees, and her mind from half forgotten beaches.

'No such luck. I expect it'll be the park, and all the sand I'll see'll be in the children's playground,' she said ruefully.

The clock in the nearby market town of Ashleigh struck four. She glanced at her watch as if unable to believe its chime.

'Heaven! I was meant to pick up Susi at quarter to four. I've got some shopping to do and Miss Atwood said I could leave early . . . '

Taking her bag from her drawer, she drew a comb quickly through the long shining fair hair, throwing it back with an impatient gesture over her shoulder. She wished now she'd had it cut at the beginning of the summer, it made her neck so hot, but who would have foretold months of hot sunshine such as they'd had.

She slipped off the sandals she wore to the office, and put on the flat heeled shoes she used for driving. Then putting the cover over her typewriter, she banged the desk drawers shut again and jumped to her feet. She flew along the corridor and down the stairs which led to Reception ... The Security Officer, Joe Crump, called after her with a grin. 'Where's the fire Mrs. Ross?'

'Nowhere I hope,' she tossed back over her shoulder as she reached the swing doors, 'I'm late picking up Susi.'

As she reached the steps, after the cool air conditioning of the building the heat from the tarmac on the car park struck her with an almost tangible force. She could imagine that Matilda, the name Susi had given their little red Mini, would be like an oven. It stood at the end of the parking lot, humble among the Jags and Mercs of some of the superior hierarchy.

As she had anticipated, opening the door of the little car was like putting her head inside a furnace. Although she only wore a light cotton dress with low cut neck and no sleeves, already she could feel the dampness start between her shoulders, and anticipated the sticky heat rising from the plastic seat.

Quickly she wound down both the windows, then started the engine and drove out from the car park to the shady lane which led up to the new carriageway.

Beresford's block of modern offices stood a few miles out of Ashleigh, built near the quarry which was only part of the huge complex of businesses in which David Beresford had an interest — cattle haulage, transport, building — all of them neatly tabulated, analysed, computerised and housed in the glass and concrete building. Sometimes, just thinking of all the hundreds of people and all the details involved, made Alison feel a very small cog in an enormous wheel.

She was only a typist in the general office, copy typist and filing clerk, one of the lesser forms of human life, she told herself sometimes, half humorously. But the firm paid slightly above the norm for someone not particularly skilled, and it meant she could run the little car and that she and Susi kept their heads above water — providing nothing unforeseen happened to her or the job, the threat a brooding shadow that hovered continuously at the back of her mind . . .

The lane was dusty with lack of rain, and the lorries which came and went from the quarry below the office block made their own small dust storms every time they passed, leaving a white film over the foliage and grass of the banks and hedges.

She turned on the dual carriageway, pressing her foot down on the accelerator, her mind racing towards Susi waiting at Playschool where Alison left her little daughter during working hours.

She had a long list of shopping for the weekend in her bag, and her mind was running up and down the items like some demented squirrel, trying to eliminate those not entirely essential. She came to the turning marked Ashfield and drove swiftly towards the town. She'd been born just outside it, her father a small farmer, but both he and her mother had been killed in a car accident when she was still at school. The farm was only rented, and Alison had been brought up by a spinster aunt, a strict and God-fearing woman, kind in her way, but totally inadequate as far as a small girl and her emotional needs were concerned. She had died too when Alison was eighteen and now, apart from friends and acquaintances in the small town, where everyone knew nearly everyone else, she had no relatives.

Basically it was still a mill town producing blankets and serge and luxury carpets, surprisingly alive and virile, and its narrow streets much easier to negotiate now the by-pass had been built. At one time it had hardly been safe to walk along its pavements either side of the narrow high street, and often quite impossible to hold a normal conversation because of the noise of the traffic. There had been the occasion when someone had had the lettuce they were carrying whisked away by the traffic mirror of a passing car! But now Alison could drive swiftly along the street and turn off into a quiet road on the edge of town, shaded by sycamore trees to the old Georgian house where the Playschool was held.

Susi was sitting in the big bow window, her nose pressed against the glass as she waited. For her six years she was a surprisingly obedient and thoughtful child, and Alison knew with certainty she would be waiting where she had been told.

Now, seeing her mother, she jumped down off the window seat, waving Huggy Bear as she ran down the steps to the gate. Huggy Bear was dressed in the same blue cotton as her own dress. For a moment a little frown appeared between Alison's brows — sometimes she wondered how on earth she was ever going to prise the rather tatty teddy bear away from Susi when she went to school next term. The two were inseparable, Susi would refuse to eat or sleep unless Huggy were present . . . Alison knew life was difficult enough for a small girl with no father without the added cruelty other children could inflict over what they would probably consider a sign of babyness.

The teddy bear was very dilapidated now, most of his fur worn off, his eyes replaced by shining brown buttons, and a new ear she had had to sew on where Susi had cut her teeth on the original. To the child he was still a beloved companion.

Maybe he's some sort of compensation for the father she's never had, Alison thought with a trace of bitterness.

The child opened the car door and

climbed on to the passenger seat,

'How about Huggy's hat?' Alison smiled down at her daughter.

'He feels the heat something shocking,' Susi explained carefully, 'brown bears like it cool, Miss Thingy said . . .'

'I do wish you wouldn't use that awful expression instead of a person's proper name, Susi. She's Miss Ransome . . .'

Susi glanced sideways at her mother, and with the shrewd observation of childhood said, 'You're hot and cross like a Good Friday bun!' She giggled, 'Never mind, Huggy and I will get the tea d'rectly we get home, and you can kick off your shoes and put up your feet. Then I'll change into my Peanuts shirt, my shorts and flip flaps — Huggy can go naked, 'cept for his fur, what's left of it. Then we'll all feel better.'

Alison felt a stab of guilt. Tiredness sometimes made her sharp with Susi, she regretted it immediately, it was so unfair . . . She patted the bare knee, 'O.K. love, sorry about the hot-cross bit, we've been awfully busy at the

9

office, and it is terribly hot . . . '

'Poor Mum,' the child said softly. Her eyes held an adult understanding and depth in them when she looked at her mother . . . maybe she'd been thrust into the outside world too soon. Now she chatted away nineteen to the dozen, talking about the other kids, some of whose names Alison knew, others she'd never heard of.

'Who's Janice?' she asked, her mind only partly on what Susi was talking about, mostly still with her shopping list. The stores seemed to close earlier and earlier, essentials got more and more expensive, and in this heat food just didn't keep. She only had a tiny fridge, bought second-hand and constantly on the blink. Often she dreamed of the luxury of a deep-freeze. As it was, life was a constant battle to keep milk fresh, meat from going off and bread from growing the green mould, which seemed peculiar to it nowadays.

Susi went on, 'Oh you know Janice Mum, her front teeth fell out that lunch time, I told you . . . ' her voice was just a little plaintive.

Alison nodded absently. In some ways Susi had grown up in the time she'd been at Playschool, been absorbed into a little world that Alison wasn't part of any more, but it was part of the price she had to pay, spending so many hours away from the small child, missing so much of her babyhood, knowing there were experiences she would never share . . .

If only . . . the two saddest words in the English language — if only she were a normal married woman with a home and husband — the proper background for a child to grow up in . . .

She pulled herself up sharply. In lots of ways she was lucky, much luckier than many women you heard of and read about. It wasn't as if she was a teenager, mooning over what might have been. She was twenty-eight . . .

And then suddenly the long empty years stretched ahead — empty that is apart from Susi. So often now she thought that a child, for the first five years of its life, needed its mother totally — like a shadow that only left her when she went to bed — and yet her little girl seemed to have survived without too much damage — apart from the fact of clinging to Huggy Bear — and maybe that was natural . . .

She always took Susi round the supermarket with her, which made the going slow, particularly as she was weighed down by Huggy Bear, but she quelled the first irritation that sometimes she felt at the delay, it was only fair the few hours they had together that at least they should spend all they could in each other's company, even if it was only dragging round the supermarket before it closed.

Susi pushed the wire trolley round the shelves, Huggy Bear sitting on the small folding seat. Alison collected tins and packets from the shelves, mentally adding up the prices as she went. Now and then Susi trailed behind, small tongue protruding through her teeth as she concentrated on negotiating the busy evening crowds doing their week-end shopping, glancing up and smiling as she said, ''Scuse me please ... ' Occasionally one of them stopped and bent down to answer her or pat Huggy Bear. Alison would feel a little surge of pride, she was such a friendly, natural child, always chatting away and yet, she hoped, good mannered ... she sighed, a tin of beans clasped in her hand, of one thing she was certain, all she'd had to do, to sacrifice, the effort and the work were more than worthwhile just to see Susi happy, to feel her soft arms round her neck and the gentle kiss like the touch of a butterfly wing on her cheek as she said, 'Mum, I love you — you and Huggy Bear are the bestest people in the whole world ... ' And sometimes when at last she'd dropped off to sleep, Alison stood looking down at her, murmuring softly ... 'and you're the best thing that ever happened to me ... '

As if she knew what her mother was

thinking, Susi glanced up as she joined her with the trolley, giving a little hiss through her teeth as she drew up.

'That's our air brakes working, Mum, like the big lorries from Beresfords . . . ' She gave a wide smile, her eyes dancing, a smile of sheer love and affection lighting up her face.

'Come on then love, we're only half way through, tell Huggy to put his paw down on the accelerator . . . '

They whizzed past the shelf of chocolate biscuits . . . and for a moment Susi's eyes lingered longingly on the Orange Milk Chocolate Sandwich packets, her favourite, and Huggy's of course. But she didn't plead or whine, she knew Alison couldn't afford luxuries . . . but now on a sudden impulse Alison reached up and tucked a packet of the biscuits behind Huggy Bear, her finger to her lips, laughing conspiratorially at the little girl. 'Sh, not a word to Huggy or he'll eat them. We'll stand ourselves a treat just this once . . . '

14

Susi threw her arms round her mother's waist, and then skipped back to her duty as trolley pusher until at last they reached the check-out desk. The long column of figures seemed more threatening than usual. Alison fished out her pay envelope and counted out the precious notes. Fortunately the store had its own car park and they could wheel the trolley right up to Matilda. Alison opened the boot and carefully they packed their purchases inside, then, Susi returned the trolley to where the others stood neatly stacked.

Now Alison thought longingly of home — even though the little flat was tiny, it *was* home and she loved it. It was in the attic of an old Georgian house and would be boiling hot and airless beneath the roof, but oh the bliss of being able to sink into the big old arm chair, kick off her shoes, and sip the long awaited cup of coffee.

She'd run some cold water over her wrists first while the coffee perked . . . wearily she lifted the hair off her neck as Susi climbed into the passenger seat, her chores done, Huggy Bear once more in her arms.

'Mum, you know Stevie, I've told you about him, what do you think he did today?' Without waiting for her mother to reply, she giggled and went on, 'he found a clown's costume in the dress-up box and then juggled with some eggs, real ones Miss Ransome was going to cook for our tea — you should have seen the mess . . . ' she stopped for a moment, watching the van in front. 'What's it say on there Mum? There's a picture of a typewriter like yours, but I can only read the big print . . . when I can really read I'll be able to tell you the stories won't I instead of the other way round, then you can rest . . . '

Alison nodded and started to read . . . 'Come to us for all your office needs . . . carbons, papers, files . . . '

Suddenly she gave a gasp of dismay . . . the Fordwell contract file . . . it was lying on her desk back at the office marked Private and Confidential, with

16

details of a quotation from Beresfords . . . as clearly as a piece of film unrolling before her eyes, she could see the fat manilla file lying by her typewriter . . .

'Susi love, I'm sorry, we're going to have to wait a bit longer for tea, I'll have to go back to the office . . . but only for a second I promise — well five minutes at the most while I put something away I forgot . . . '

For a moment the corners of Susi's mouth took a downward turn, but quickly she buried her face in Huggy Bear as Alison let in the clutch and turned swiftly back the way she had come.

Once more her mind winged ahead . . . please don't let anyone have touched the file, she prayed, don't let anyone find out I've been careless.

She swung down the lane and decided not to take the car to the park by the reception area where the sun still beat down relentlessly, she'd leave it on the edge of the entrance where a huge oak tree shed a little shade . . .

'Shan't be a moment, love . . . '

She sped across the dusty tarmac and back through the swing doors. Joe was preparing to go off duty.

'Well, what now?' he grinned, 'it isn't your day Mrs. Ross, is it?'

She shook her head, 'No . . . I just forgot something, shan't be a jiff . . . '

Her heart was in her mouth as she dashed up the stairs and flung open the office door. All was quiet, the typewriters silent under their covers, the bluebottle buzzed in the window. Her eyes flew to her own desk . . . the file still lay where she had left it. Sweet relief flooded through her. At least something had gone right with the day. The room felt odd with no clatter of typewriters, no phones ringing, no chatter and coming and going.

Quickly she put the file in the cabinet and locked it, glancing round to make sure she'd not forgotten anything else, then she ran along the corridor and down the stairs, calling good night to

Joe, hearing the low murmur of voices from behind the managing director — David Beresford's office door. He usually seemed to work late so his secretary had confided once in the canteen. It wasn't all honey being the boss, she supposed. As she reached the parking lot it still shimmered with the airless heat of the day.

She was about halfway across when she saw Huggy Bear's hat lying by the Mini . . .

Susi was strictly forbidden ever to leave the car when it was parked, specially outside Beresfords, the huge lorries and transporters that were garaged at the back of the office block, whipped down the lane as if there was no tomorrow, often turning in the car park entrance.

It was totally unlike Susi to be disobedient . . . for a moment irritation rose within her — not her too — life seemed to be crowding her — she couldn't take much more . . .

As she reached the car she saw the

door on the passenger side was open. The car was empty . . .

'Susi!' she called, turning swiftly and running out into the lane. It curved away in the dusty heat, deserted, it was almost as if it mocked her with its emptiness when she had half expected to see a small, blue clad figure . . . Not even a breeze stirred the coated leaves and grasses . . . the heavy silence that hung over everything held menace . . .

'Susi!' she cried again, an edge of hysteria creeping into her tone.

She'd only been gone five minutes at the most. The child's small legs couldn't have carried her all that far in that time . . .

She'd tried to keep control of herself, to use her common sense. Maybe she'd wanted to spend a penny and gone to look for a loo . . . maybe she's playing a game . . . it's not like her . . . normally she does as she's told, she's always only too anxious not to cause me any anxiety . . . she told herself.

Glancing round there was nowhere

she could see where she might have hidden.

Frantically she dashed up the lane, calling over and over again, tears of fear and frustration pouring down her cheeks. She could feel the damp sweat as her thin dress stuck to her back.

On the road the cars tore by, unheeding, trailing lorries, hooting impatiently . . .

There was no sign anywhere of a small girl in a blue dress . . .

Suffocating panic rose inside her. She had never been so frightened and desperate in her whole life . . .

2

Alison stood uncertainly on the scorched verge of the road. It was as though her limbs were paralysed. The whoosh of passing cars made her sway slightly as they whizzed by.

She couldn't think clearly. She just didn't know what to do next, whom to turn to . . .

The police . . . a phone . . .

She raced back to Reception once more.

Joe had changed from his uniform, the night watchman was about to relieve him.

Seeing her white face the security man stepped forward. Alison was so breathless now she could hardly form the words . . .

'It's Susi . . . my little girl . . . she's gone . . . ' The information jerked out from her.

'Gone?' Joe puckered his brow . . .

'Yes . . . from the car where I left her . . . '

He put his hand on her arm. 'Don't get upset Mrs. Ross, I expect she's hiding, you know what kids are. Probably got fed up waiting . . . '

Alison shook her head, 'I've looked everywhere, anyway she never leaves the car, she knows she mustn't . . . '

'Come on, love,' he pushed her gently towards the door, 'let's have another look, kids will be kids.'

Alison followed him back to the Mini. She seemed to have lost the power of self motivation, she was walking in the quality of a nightmare . . .

Joe peered over the hedge into a nearby field, searched an old tin roofed shed which leant drunkenly at the side of the oak tree, which Alison hadn't noticed.

They both shouted Susi's name — but only silence, the distant hum of traffic, and a mocking crow in the tree top, answered them.

Suddenly Alison felt an icy calm. She took a grip on herself. 'I'm going to ring the police.' When a child disappeared, that was the obvious thing to do — get in touch with the police . . .

David Beresford had had a trying day. Several small things had annoyed him, in the intense heat of the August day they had become magnified out of all proportion.

His secretary was on holiday and she'd left a 'temp' who had come with glowing references from an employment agency. Her shorthand and typing were indeed faultless, but she was like a well designed machine, unless you 'programmed' her with the information you needed, she didn't have to have any answers, no initiative — and he admired initiative in others above all, it was how he'd built up his own business.

On top of all that some idiot had run into his car on the motorway yesterday as he was returning from a conference in London, just at the time his second car had gone in for service, which meant he had to rely on his daughter Sarah to pick him up — and Sarah wasn't too keen on being tied to specific times and places . . .

So now, when he heard some kind of commotion occurring outside his office in the Reception area, he felt all the bottled up irritations rising like an irresistible force inside him.

He hesitated a moment, glancing in the mirror that hung above the drinks cabinet, straightened his tie, brushing back a lock of the dark hair that would not stay in place in spite of all the efforts of both himself and his barber . . . there were only scattered grey hairs among the dark curls, and his blue eyes were bright and alert, his figure no disgrace to a man ten years younger than himself. He looked at his watch — just after five — Sarah would be on her way now he hoped — at least that would mean a cool drink when he got home. Maybe he could put his feet up for half an hour and listen to some Mozart . . . he hummed a few bars to calm himself — which piano concerto should he choose, what was suitable for a hot summer evening . . . maybe Debussey would be better . . .

He thrust open the door. A little knot of people stood in the lobby. The centre of their interest appeared to be a girl, about the same age as Sarah he guessed from what he could see. She was so excited as to be almost hysterical . . . he sighed . . . oh dear . . . he'd seen her somewhere before, he couldn't remember exactly where, he supposed she must be one of the office staff . . . the incident was adding to his annoyance. Usually he was good at remembering faces, and putting names to them, you had to be in his business.

The girl had a thick mane of golden hair flowing over her shoulders — most of them had these days — now it was pulled back from her face, tucked back behind her ears anyhow, he could see she was pale, her cheeks tear stained. She seemed to be asking Joe to phone the police, a torrent of words fell at

26

random from her lips. The night watchman stood by as if hypnotised by all that was going on.

At that moment the outside door was pushed open and his daughter Sarah with his grandchild, Jo-Anne, came in. They stopped short when they saw the scene. Then the girl by the phone turned towards Sarah, talking fast and waving her arms about, pointing out towards the car park . . .

Slowly now, and rather unwillingly, he approached them. He didn't really want to get involved, drawn into whatever was happening, he just wanted to go home and relax. But he knew he had no alternative, this was his building, his business, he was the boss and must take charge . . .

As his footsteps sounded on the polished tiles of the floor, the eyes of the various people turned towards him.

For a moment there was a pause, the silence broken only by the whirring of the dial on the phone. Then Sarah said to the girl —

'But she can't have just disappeared surely, how long did you leave her?'

And the girl replied, 'I know it seems ridiculous, that's what I keep telling myself, but I've looked everywhere, and Joe has . . . I only slipped up to the office . . . ' she broke off as she became aware of David's presence, and her voice trailed off into silence.

Maybe some sixth sense had warned her that even in this crisis she should not advertise the fact of her own carelessness and forgetfulness. Her job was all that stood between Susi and herself and unemployment . . .

Briefly now the night watchman explained to David what had happened . . .

He turned to the girl and asked gently, 'Where exactly did you leave the car?'

She explained 'It was the only bit of shade you see and the car was so hot — and Susi . . . '

David broke in. 'I don't quite understand why the little girl was left, in fact why she was here at all — and was she likely to go off on her own?'

Alison shook her head. 'No, that's just the point, she never got out of the car when I left it . . . I work in the typing pool, and I came back just for a moment because I'd forgotten something, I'd picked Susi up from Playschool . . . ' Once more the tears started to run down her cheeks.

Then they all swung round to look at the door as a car drew up outside and a young policeman got out of a Panda, coming swiftly through the swing door. David could see that Alison was near collapse, white and trembling . . . he put out his hand.

'Let's go to my office my dear, you can sit down there and tell the constable all about it . . . '

He guided her to the nearest chair and she sank down, dropping her head on her hands . . .

Sarah and Jo-Anne had followed him, standing hesitantly for a moment, looking at the policeman. Then the little girl ran to her grandfather, clasping him round the waist and looking up at him . . .

'Grandy, I've been in the pool all afternoon. Mummy said I needn't go to silly old school, it was too hot. Are you coming to have a swim now?'

He bent down and lifted her into his arms. 'Why not Jo-Jo? I agree it's too hot to do anything else.'

Sarah glanced at her diamond studded watch. 'Are you ready then, Pop? I've got people coming for a party at half past six, we'll need the pool . . . '

The policeman cleared his throat. 'Which is the young lady who reported a lost child?' He looked from Alison to Sarah and down at Jo-Anne.

David put the child down and gave her a gentle push towards her mother, nodding his head as if in dismissal.

'I must see what I can do here first, of course.'

He turned to Alison, who had managed to compose herself a little.

'I'm so sorry, I didn't catch your name . . .'

'Mrs. Ross, Alison Ross.' She glanced at the policeman, 'It's Susi, my little girl . . .'

Briefly she answered his questions — what Susi looked like, what she was wearing . . . 'She's got plaits, fair hair, a snub nose . . . and a bear, a teddy bear, she never goes anywhere without it . . . that's the first thing I noticed, his hat, on the ground, and the car door left open as if she'd gone in a hurry . . .'

The policeman wrote it down in his book. He gave an involuntary sigh. Disappearing kids were almost as frequent an occurrence as heath fires had been during this long hot summer. Usually they ended up by being found at the house of a friend, or had followed a dog or cat — the mother always swore it was the last thing they'd do, that they never moved, were models of obedience . . . it seemed nearly every day of the week he, or one of his mates, was

31

following up runaways from teenagers down to those who could just toddle out of an inviting open garden gate . . . if only they would think ahead a bit, these mothers, use some common sense . . .

'She's six — seven next month,' Alison replied in answer to more questions, all of which seemed to her nothing but a waste of time . . .

As he wrote, the phone rang, making her jump. Instinctively she got to her feet as if some magic had brought Susi to the other end of the instrument . . . David lifted the receiver.

'Beresford here. Who is this?'

The other people in the room were half listening, half pretending not to be taking any notice of what might be a private conversation. It seemed the caller was doing all the talking and had a lot to say.

As David listened his expression changed . . . for a moment, unbelievably, it was almost as though he were scared by what he heard. His eyes flew to where Jo-Anne and Sarah stood by the door waiting for him as if to reassure himself they were flesh and blood . . . relief replaced the fear as he said tersely, his hand over the mouthpiece.

'Quiet please, all of you.' The voice held the authority of a man used to being obeyed, and now his face was grim as he listened . . . then he said, 'I don't quite follow you. Who exactly is this calling?'

There was a pause once more, the listeners in the room tense now, edgy with curiosity and the first faint stirrings of apprehension . . . The voice the other end could be heard more clearly, although the words themselves were not audible.

Then David said, 'You'll do what?'

More words followed, then as if he were repeating instructions, he said, 'You'll contact me at my house, at Woodrising, at ten o'clock? Very well . . . I shall be waiting.'

There was a faint click as the receiver

the other end was replaced. Alison had sunk into the chair again, disinterested now the call had obviously no connection with Susi. She sat immobile, hardly part of the scene at all, going over in her mind what she had told the policeman, trying to make sure she had told him every detail that might be of use, anxious only now for some action to be taken . . . at once . . .

David turned to the policeman. 'I'd like to talk to you outside for a moment, constable.'

Alison looked at him sharply. 'Please, can't it wait, please let him start to look for Susi without any more time wasted.'

David nodded, 'In a moment that is exactly what we will do, but I can promise you it is important that I have just a word with him first . . . '

Their voices came distantly from outside the half closed door. Jo-Anne fidgeted, Sarah lit a cigarette, uncertain what there was she could do or say to comfort this girl, Alison . . .

She held out the packet of cigarettes.

Alison shook her head. 'No thank you.'

Sarah picked up the internal phone on her father's desk, 'I'll see if we can get some coffee from the canteen . . .'

But before she could dial the number David and the policeman came back into the room. Their faces were grim. David went over to Alison, taking Sarah's arm and drawing her with him to stand by her.

'Mrs. Ross,' he said gently, 'please listen to me very carefully. You're going to have to be very brave and sensible . . . whoever was on the other end of that telephone line — and understandably he prefers to remain anonymous — he has just told me that he has kidnapped my granddaughter, Jo-Anne Leach, and that she will be perfectly safe providing we follow his instructions to the letter, these are to be telephoned later to my house . . .'

Alison stared up at him, her expression blank, her eyes lifeless. All this delay, this talk, when all she wanted was to find Susi, to go home, for life to be normal again instead of this bizarre nightmare into which she had been thrust. What he was saying didn't really register — if something had happened to his grandchild, then she was sorry of course — but at the moment she could only think of her own trouble . . .

For a moment there was complete silence as all eyes turned towards Jo-Anne, and the child, as she felt their scrutiny, thinking she had done something wrong, puckered up her small face and started to whimper . . .

Alison started to speak . . . 'But . . . I don't quite understand . . . '

David broke in, 'You don't understand any more than I did at first . . . but you see you drive the same colour car as Sarah — a scarlet Mini. It was parked outside just at the time Sarah was due to pick me up. The kidnappers must have known this, planned it all carefully, even known my car was out of commission . . . you see at first glance the two cars would be identical. A little girl was sitting just

where she was supposed — expected
— to be . . . '

Alison gazed up at him. Her mind
refused to accept what he was saying
. . . The word 'kidnappers' was all that
seemed to register in her utter confusion — and now it hung in letters of fire
between her and David . . .

He went on slowly, almost reluctantly, 'Don't you see — an identical
situation — only it was the wrong Mini
— and the wrong little girl . . . '

3

'The wrong little girl . . . '

The words ran round and round in Alison's brain. It was as though some disembodied voice were repeating them over and over again . . . 'the wrong little girl.'

David Beresford had uttered the words — at least she thought he had, her mind was so confused . . . 'the wrong Mini and the wrong little girl . . . '

It sounded so impersonal . . . but that wrong little girl was Susi, her baby — no, not a baby, a little girl.

She shut her eyes, willing herself not to cry, squeezing the lids together.

Maybe when she opened them Susi would be there, Huggy Bear in her arms, grinning up at her, eyes crinkling at the corners like her father's used to . . .

Someone spoke to her. She forced open her lids which felt as if they had lead weights on them. David stood in front of her, a glass of dark liquid in his hand.

'Mrs. Ross, try to drink this.'

She shook her head. It wasn't that she never drank — not that she liked it much — but she wanted to try to keep her thoughts clear . . .

He persisted, 'Please believe me, brandy is a good kind of medicine at a time like this.' He tried to smile but it was a bleak attempt.

She put out her hand and took the glass. It was easier than resisting.

He went back to the drinks cabinet and poured himself a stiff whisky.

The neat spirit burnt her throat, making her choke, making the tears already in her eyes, spill down her cheeks. She had no idea of how much time had passed since that terrible moment when she realised Susi was missing — it could be hours or minutes.

She glanced round, the room seemed to be full of people. Sarah stood close beside her, the Security man and the nightwatchman were still by the phone, the young policeman with his notebook in his hand . . . but now there were two other strangers — men in dark suits, one young, one middle aged . . . She felt detached, almost lightheaded as she looked at them all . . . maybe it was the brandy . . .

She looked up at the man standing above her.

'Detective Inspector Bond, Mrs. Ross,' he turned and indicated the younger man, 'and this is Detective Sergeant Mitchell . . . now I'd be glad if you'd tell us just in your own words, briefly what happened. Take your time, but try not to leave out anything, the smallest detail which may not seem important to you . . . where you left your little girl, for how long and so on. If you saw anyone . . . anyone at all, even someone you perhaps might not particularly notice — like say one of the

40

workmen or staff from here — a driver, anyone . . .'

Alison looked up at him, shaking her head. 'No, I didn't see anyone . . .'

'Please try to think — it could be important . . .'

Suddenly she got to her feet. 'I can't tell you any more than I've already told everyone else — at least it seems like everyone,' her voice broke. 'Please, for goodness sake, why aren't you doing something.' She knew she sounded hysterical, but it seemed like hours now since Susi had disappeared, and all anyone had done was talk . . . talk . . .

The young Sergeant stepped forward and put out his hand, touching her arm. 'Look Mrs. Ross, I understand exactly how you feel — I've got a kid myself, just about your Susi's age — mine's a boy though,' he grinned, 'thing is they do the darndest things — and as you told the constable your Susi is usually pretty obedient and wouldn't get out of the car — you see we have to ask all these questions because it could be that whoever took her away was someone she knew — someone who said they had come from you even — that's why although we seem a bit slow, we do have to ask all these questions.'

For a moment Alison swayed as though she were about to fall, the glass of brandy fell from her hand, the glass tinkling against the small table as the liquid spread — a dark stain on the thick carpet. The sergeant put his arm round her to steady her.

Thankfully, she leant against him, her legs like jelly.

'Thanks, I do understand, but I just can't tell you any more than I already have . . .'

He nodded, and the Inspector went on, 'What we would like you to do Mrs. Ross, is to go back with Mr. Beresford to his house, and wait there, if you could, please . . .'

She looked at him with surprise. 'But surely . . . I mean I thought you'd want me down at the police station . . . that I could stay there while you look for Susi . . . '

He shook his head. 'No. You see it's more than likely up to now — unless they have any reason to think otherwise — they still believe they have Mr. Beresford's granddaughter . . . '

'But I don't see what difference that makes . . . can't I go to my own flat then?' She felt the sudden need to be among her own familiar surroundings . . . not in some alien place.

The Inspector's voice held a note of impatience. Kidnapping cases were rare in his neck of the woods — in fact he'd only ever dealt with one before, and that had been in the Midlands where he'd worked prior to being drafted to the west country. He knew the procedure well enough, but usually at least there was some kind of rhyme or reason. This seemed odd — a small-time typist having her child kidnapped, could it simply be a domestic affair of some kind — a jealous boy friend or husband — or was it a genuine mistake that had been made . . . if they had intended to take Beresford's grandchild — well the reason could well be cash.

It was common knowledge Beresford was a rich man — but surely even he couldn't produce enough money to make the risk kidnapping held worthwhile . . .

Anyway, whatever the ins and outs of it, the quicker they got the whole thing cleared up the better, the public got very edgy with the police in these kinds of cases if something wasn't done — and seen to be done — quickly . . . must keep it from the press at all costs . . .

He gave Alison a little push towards David . . . 'Mr. Beresford, perhaps you'd be kind enough to drive Mrs. Ross to your home, and meet the Sergeant and myself there.' He turned to Alison. 'Meanwhile Mrs. Ross, we shall have to take your car I'm afraid, it must be tested for fingerprints and so on . . . ' And, he added to himself, you are in no fit state to drive, young woman . . . emotionally disturbed . . .

He sighed. This was going to be a long and tedious business, he could feel it in his bones, and he was tired, his ulcer had been playing him up again, and somehow young Mitchell's keenness and what he considered to be rather emotional approach, irritated him. It was always best not to get emotionally involved. He considered the police image of the present day was sloppy, slack . . . not as it had been when he was young, and the public had more respect for the law, and its administrators. It annoyed him, undermined his authority that he was known as 'James' Bond to his colleagues, although actually his name was John . . . he knew too that behind his back they referred to him as 006½ — a kind of parody on 007, the original James Bond of Ian Fleming . . . he liked a set of rules and to stick to them — but today it was the fashion not to work by the book as he'd been taught . . .

David took Alison's hand in his. 'I'm

sorry I haven't my own car, but Sarah will drive us to Woodrising, and perhaps on the way you'd like to collect some things from your own flat, Mrs. Ross.' He turned to the Inspector, 'I imagine that will be in order?'

The Inspector nodded.

David took charge naturally — this was his domain, his little kingdom. It needed organisation, and that was something he could do. He could understand how this girl felt, police methods were slow, ponderous, and secretly he hadn't much time for this Inspector Bond, he struck him as being a blundering old fool . . . now the young Sergeant was a different kettle of fish. He hoped he'd be the one to handle most of the details.

He held open the door of the little red Mini, while Alison climbed into the back. It wasn't really much like her own now she saw it closely, except in colour . . . it was a current model, gleaming and immaculate, whereas poor old Matilda, who still stood under the oak tree where she had parked it, was shabby and battered.

For a moment a sob caught in her throat looking at the lonely little car, and the policeman about to drive it away — adding to the bleak misery in her heart.

David got in beside Sarah and the young Sergeant lifted Jo-Anne on to his knee.

'We'll follow you, sir, I've made arrangements for a tape recorder to be brought to your house . . . ' He bent his head and looked at Alison on the back seat. 'We want to make sure we have a record of their voices, Mrs. Ross. It might be that you could recognise something about them . . . '

She looked at him in bewilderment. She still couldn't understand why it was so necessary for her to go to the Beresford house, surely she should be at home where they would return Susi when they found out the whole thing had been a terrible mistake . . .

Seeing her confusion he went on

gently, 'You see, they may want to speak to you — usually it is the mother they want to contact . . . '

'How soon will they know they have the wrong child?' As she uttered the words she knew of course it was a question he couldn't possibly answer . . . but Mitchell showed no impatience — he knew this kind of stunned disbelief was the first characteristic reaction of one whose wife, or child or husband had met with some terrible occurrence — a disbelief that it could possibly be true, dulling the usual intelligence — sometimes even so acute it crowded out grief — it might even be days before the facts of death, injury or kidnapping could be realised, let alone accepted — all this went through his mind as he looked at her — it would not have probably occurred to his superior — as David had surmised, Mitchell and Bond were as different as violin strings and a ploughshare . . .

'Fairly quickly I expect, your little girl sounds unusually bright . . . '

A ray of hope stirred faintly. 'Then perhaps . . . I mean . . . they'll let her go as soon as they realise — at once — there'd be no point in keeping her when they find out it isn't Mr. Beresford's grandchild, would there?'

It was as if she willed him to reassure her . . . to agree . . .

For a moment his eyes wavered at her gaze . . . he stood back abruptly from the window, clearing his throat . . . he guessed she knew as well as he did the implications — the child had seen the kidnappers — could describe them . . .

Now Alison leant forward, sick panic rising once more, her eyes darting in desperation from David's face to the Sergeant's . . . 'They won't . . . they wouldn't . . . ' She couldn't bring her lips to form the words . . . for the first time the real and ghastly truth of what the kidnappers might well do when they found out it wasn't Jo-Anne they had was driven home as she saw the expression in the two men's eyes as she glanced hopelessly from one to the other, trying to discern a ray of hope, of reassurance . . . she fell back against the seat then, her eyes closed, feeling faint . . . dizzy . . .

Sarah drove swiftly in the direction Alison herself had driven earlier. David gave her brief instructions — he knew exactly where she lived. At the time it didn't seem odd, nothing really registered, it wasn't till much later she discovered he'd got her file from personnel with his master key . . . the Inspector had wanted to see it — and so now he could direct Sarah to the house the other side of town.

Apart from his few terse words, no one spoke . . . even Jo-Anne seemed subdued by the mood of her elders . . .

As the car drew up outside the gate, she stumbled to her feet, David held the seat forward, clasping her arm, and for a moment the slight pressure of his fingers brought a little comfort to the coldness which seemed to wrap around her in spite of the airless heat of the evening . . .

She opened the street door with her key, leaning for a moment against the lintel. She felt suddenly desperately tired and old . . .

Sarah had followed her. She stood now watching her, feeling helpless, inadequate . . . all her life she'd been shielded, protected from the outside world, cushioned by her father's money and affection. Now she stood looking at this girl who wasn't much older than she was, this girl who could have been her, whose child had been snatched instead of her own. She just didn't know what to do to help, to get through to her, they lived in different worlds . . . and yet they had the bond of motherhood . . . she wondered where the husband was, no one had mentioned him . . . so she presumed the girl was on her own . . . a widow, divorced, deserted perhaps . . . that made it even worse . . .

Alison was scarcely aware of Sarah's presence. She seemed only to be able to absorb one thing at a time, take one

51

step as though she were crippled
. . . Now she knew she had to collect a
few things she would need for the night
— only one night, tomorrow Susi
would be back . . . she must just find
what she needed, put it into some kind
of case . . . she didn't remember if she
had a suitcase, she and Susi never went
away . . . maybe her shopping holdall
. . . then she remembered that was still
in the boot of Matilda with the week
end shopping in it . . .

She made her way up the narrow
stairs that led to the attic, and Sarah
followed, taking in the dingy walls, the
torn lino, and then glancing round the
tiny flat as Alison opened the door.
There were books, photos, a few
pictures and posters that Susi had
pasted up . . . for a moment they stood,
one behind the other, just looking
. . . Alison saw all the reminders of her
little girl that lay around . . . she
thought with a pain in her heart of the
times she'd been impatient, short with
her . . . her shoes, scuffed and shabby,

lay where she had kicked them off under the table, the snakes and ladders board with the half finished game they'd been playing last night, the bikini she'd made for Huggy Bear to match Susi's own. The two neat beds in the corner where Susi lay tucked up at night while Alison read to her . . .

A sob escaped her. Sarah put out her hand awkwardly . . .

'Look, can I collect a few things for you . . . '

Alison shook her head, 'No, thanks all the same, I'll be all right . . . and it'll be quicker if I do it myself . . . '

Now as Sarah gazed round at the shabby bits and pieces, the home-made curtains, the patched covers on the chairs, she thought of her own rooms at Woodrising, where she and Brian lived in the flat her father had had made for them when they married, the luxurious carpets, the tiled bathroom, the hot house flowers . . . a little gasp of pity escaped her . . . Alison glanced at her. 'What's the matter?'

'I'm sorry, but it just struck me, it must be pretty tough, bringing up a kid in these kind of surroundings, under these conditions . . . ' she broke off quickly. 'I didn't . . . I don't mean that rudely — please don't take offence, it's just that I never realised before how darned lucky I am to have Daddy to make things easy for me . . . it suddenly came home to me . . . '

Alison realised she hadn't meant to be unkind . . . Sarah had felt an overwhelming need to atone somehow for the yawning gap in their lives . . . 'I mean . . . ' she went on slowly, 'it seems so unfair that you've had all this to cope with, and then on top of it, this new thing — this awful thing — which was really meant to happen to me anyway . . . somehow I feel almost guilty about it.'

Alison gave a ghost of a smile. 'Well it isn't exactly your fault is it? I wouldn't wish it on anyone, I mean in your place I couldn't help being glad it wasn't my child, however sorry

I felt for the other person . . . '

She'd crammed a few things into a small canvas hold-all Susi sometimes took to school with a change of clothes when it was wet. Sarah took it from her, even that little gesture of help, of caring, did a bit towards salving her conscience . . .

They went back down the stairs and out into the blinding heat of the August evening to where David waited with Jo-Anne — and to Sarah it seemed her daughter had suddenly become more precious in the face of what had happened to this girl — of whose existence even she had been unaware until a few hours ago . . .

4

Alison sat on the sofa in the spacious lounge at Woodrising. She was scarcely conscious of her surroundings, had moved mechanically, done as she was told like a puppet whose strings of motivation were pulled by others . . .

She stared straight ahead of her, trying to grasp what was happening . . . most important of all, what might happen to Susi — and there her mind refused to function, appalled by the facts too awful to contemplate.

Men moved about the room, installing a tape recorder, pulling at wires, disconnecting this, connecting that, talking all the time in low voices . . . 'it's just as though someone has already died,' she thought. Bells rang, people came and went. It all washed around her like the waves of the sea against a heedless rock.

The Inspector and David Beresford were by the window where the telephone stood on a small table.

David was only half listening to what the policeman was saying, his eyes constantly returning to where Alison sat crouched on the sofa, her eyes moving restlessly, she reminded him of a terrified hare he had once seen, hearing the hounds in the distance, on its trail . . . he had to admire the very way she had behaved during the short time he had been with her . . . after the understandable emotion she had shown when the truth had dawned on her, she had seemed to take a tight rein on herself with a cool detachment, but he realised that inwardly she must feel like a tightly coiled spring. He wondered how Sarah would have behaved in like circumstances, if indeed what the kidnappers had intended had become fact and it had been Jo-Anne who had been snatched.

Of course he had to admit to an immense feeling of relief that it wasn't his granddaughter who was missing, he had a deep and tender affection for her — all he had felt at first had been a mild irritation at the upheaval, the intrusion into his usually smooth running, efficiently managed life. He liked things to go as planned, both in the office, where his personal assistant, the unflappable Miss Anderson smoothed every wrinkle out of his working hours — and at home Mrs. Finlay, his housekeeper who had been with him since his wife, Joy, died giving birth to Sarah. She had come as nurse, and now looked after the house as if it were her own. She too saw to it that the irritations of day to day living touched him as little as possible . . . oh yes, efficient business tycoon he might be, but he was sensible enough to realise much of it was due to the smoothing of his path by those around him.

Now he was landed with something quite out of his province, he didn't resent it but other, unaccustomed feelings were starting to form in his mind — and a deep compassion for this girl . . .

Inspector Bond was droning on, showing him how the tape recorder worked, how it was fixed to the telephone . . . 'Now, Sir, when the kidnappers ring, it is most important to keep them talking as long as you possibly can . . . partly because it gives us more of a chance of being able to trace the call, but mostly because often a voice can give someone away just as surely as a fingerprint. We have experts who can read these recordings . . . ' His tone annoyed David, although he realised the man was only doing his job. He had a condescending manner of talking as though explaining the whole thing to a child . . .

'Yes, yes, Inspector, I am quite aware of that fact, and I'll do my best, though I imagine the modern kidnapper, through the help of television, is as astute as your people over these matters, and knows only too well what is happening.'

He broke off as Mrs. Finlay came in with a tray of coffee and sandwiches. He introduced her to Alison saying:

'Mrs. Ross will be staying with us for a little while . . . perhaps when she has had something to eat you'd show her the spare room?'

If Louisa Finlay thought it odd that a young woman who was obviously David's friend and not Sarah's, should suddenly become part of the household, she didn't show it, she smiled at Alison. 'Of course, you just let me know when you're ready . . . '

Alison returned the smile automatically. Everyone was being very kind, as helpful as they could, like one was to those who had been bereaved . . . She felt hopeless, totally alone without Susi . . . and all the coming and going and preparations didn't seem to be helping in any way to find her. Her nerves felt raw as if they were exposed to bitter elements. It was all she could do not to open her mouth and give vent to the piercing sounds within. She wasn't even sure how long it would be before she did, how much control she had left.

As if he sensed her feelings, David now came over and sat beside her on the sofa. He poured the coffee, strong and black, and handed it to her. She sipped the scalding liquid, thankfully he didn't speak. She was conscious however that he was watching her closely, his eyes following hers as they glanced through the window.

She must show some gratitude, some thanks, even if only to remark on the beauty and luxury surrounding her . . .

'How green the grass is,' she said softly, 'still green . . . Susi'll love to watch that sprinkler — all the tiny rainbows the drops make . . . ' She spoke deliberately, determined to ignore the possibility — the probability she might not come . . . as much to reassure herself as for any other reason, speaking her thoughts aloud . . . 'and the roses, I can smell them,

and the geraniums and heliotrope
. . . I used to call it cherry pie — we
had flowers like that on the farm when
I was a child . . . '

For a moment he visualised her bare
foot, tanned, running through dewy
meadows at dawn . . . laughing . . . he
wondered how her face would look
when she laughed . . .

She put down the cup and went
slowly across to the french windows,
looking out at the shady trees casting
their evening shadows.

There was a manicured tennis
court, neatly marked out, the net
taut as if someone were going to play
and had changed their minds — the
water in the swimming pool
shimmered blue among the gaily
coloured umbrellas, and the gently
moving swing seat with a striped
canopy . . .

'How Susi will love it all . . . '

He got up and came over to where
she stood, longing to be able to say
something of comfort, to say, 'Perhaps

by this time tomorrow she'll be swimming in the pool with Jo-Anne . . . '

But the words stuck in his throat . . .

Instinctively she guessed that he knew how she was feeling.

It was strange, she felt a much deeper affinity with him than with Sarah, who was after all another woman, a mother, and much closer to her in age . . . and yet although she had been sympathetic and anxions to help, there was something about this older man that seemed to communicate with her, to bring a measure of comfort even in the darkness that surrounded her.

She was vaguely conscious of Sarah in the hall behind her, using the other phone to cancel the party she had arranged. Then she brought Brian, her husband in, to meet Alison. He was a director of Beresfords and she'd seen him once or twice in the corridors. He was a pleasant young man with a ready smile, he held her hand briefly between his, 'I'm so very sorry about your little girl, Mrs. Ross, I wish there

was something I . . . we . . . could do
. . . is there anything you need, anything
I can get . . . ' She shook her head
slowly . . . she didn't really want
anything or anyone — only Susi
. . . and now she felt David's hand on
hers, warm, soft and comforting. He
smiled as she looked at him . . .

'The waiting's the worst part, but
once they ring, then at least we'll know
something and the police will have
some facts to work on. I know it
isn't much help to keep telling you
everything'll be all right — it's easy to
say the words, but not easy to believe
them. I can guess how you feel, please
believe me, I shall do everything in my
power, just as I would if it had been
Jo-Anne . . . '

If only they'd ring . . .

He glanced at his watch. 'Only about
an hour and a half, if they keep to their
word. Why don't you go along with
Mrs. Finlay and have a freshen up. I'm
sure it would make you feel a bit
better.'

Thankful to have something concrete to do, she followed the housekeeper up the wide shallow stairs. Mrs. Finlay opened a door to the right of the landing. The room was decorated in cool shades of blue with matching, flowered chintz covers and curtains and a thick dark blue carpet. Another door opened the far side into a bathroom, she could see it was tiled from floor to ceiling too in pale blue, blue towels hung on rails, even the soap and the bath oil were coloured to match. She had never seen such comfort and luxury . . .

Two long windows opened on to a small balcony above the terrace, and away in the distance she could see the tors and foothills of the Moor . . .

For a moment she stood looking across the summer landscape, and without speaking, Mrs. Finlay opened the case and spread the few poor pathetic belongings she had brought, on the bed . . . then she went out and softly closed the door behind her.

Turning, Alison caught sight of herself in the long mirror of the built-in cupboard. She looked at the pale face and crumpled dress — no wonder David had tactfully suggested she would like to freshen up. She looked like some kind of scarecrow . . . what Susi called a Tattie Boggle . . . the thought broke down the last of her defences, and she threw herself on the softness of the bed, burying her face in the shiny chintz cover as long, shuddering sobs shook her whole body . . .

For how long she cried she had no idea, but at last it seemed as if all sorrow, and feeling was spent, had flowed from her with the tears. She was drained, empty . . .

As she dragged herself up from the bed there was a soft tap on the door. She called, 'Come in . . . ' as she did so endeavouring to smooth the creases from her dress. Sarah put her head round the door, giving a hesitant smile.

'Sorry to barge in, but I thought this might be useful . . . I realised you only brought a few things for the night, but it's been so hot and sticky and I thought if you had a shower you might like a clean dress . . . it's only a cotton sun dress, but I guess we're just about the same size . . . ' She looked at Alison's slim figure and added ruefully, 'I don't know though, in the places that matter you look a lot thinner than me. Doesn't seem to matter how much I diet, I just put on pounds . . . '

She held out a cotton dress in bright colours which Alison could tell at a glance from the design and cut, must have cost at least a week's salary as far as she was concerned. She was about to shake her head, but she thought how ungracious a gesture it would be, the girl was only trying to help, to be friendly, and from what she had seen of Sarah she imagined that to be that thoughtful had cost her quite an effort, she who had most things done for her.

She smiled. 'Thanks, it would make a difference to get out of this. I feel as if I'd slept in it.' She took the dress, feeling the soft texture of the material.

For a moment Sarah stood awkwardly, not sure what to say, what to do, like her father, the situation was out of her province, the kind of thing one read about but never actually became a personal issue.

She turned towards the door. 'Well, I'll leave you to shower and change. Jo-Anne's playing up so I'll have to go and read to her till she drops off . . .' Suddenly realising with a new awareness of other people's feelings, she felt it was tactless to have mentioned her own little girl to someone who had lost hers — she said quickly. 'If there's anything else you want, anything at all, just give a shout . . .'

Swiftly she opened the door and went out, relieved that she'd done what she intended without having to cope with any kind of scene . . .

Alison stood for a moment after she'd gone, then she laid the dress on the bed, took off her own crumpled one and went into the bathroom, pushing

68

back the damp hair from her face, pulling on the shower cap which hung with the towels, and tucking in her long fair hair. She let the warm water run over her naked body, holding up her face to it, with the swollen eyes and puffed lids, its gentle caress a sweet benison . . .

She rubbed herself dry with the luxurious deep piled towel and as she went back into the bedroom she could hear people moving about in other parts of the house, voices called and answered, there was a low laugh, a snatch of music . . . how could anyone laugh at a time like this, how could the world go on, just uncaring . . .

She pulled herself up sharply. She was being selfish, thoughtless. Life had to go on, people were doing all they could. It was just that she couldn't face the thought of living without Susi . . . it was the awful waiting, the imaginings of what might be happening to her little girl that thronged her mind. She drew on the dress. It was a little too big in places as Sarah had thought, but she drew it in with the belt and anyway it looked better than the one she had discarded, the softness and beauty of line were something she had never possessed or been able to afford. She combed her hair, put on some lipstick, dabbed powder on her red and shining nose . . . as she surveyed her reflection in the mirror she heard a car drive up with a crunch of gravel below the window.

She went over and looked down into the gathering summer twilight, her heart quickening as a gleam of hope that it might be someone bringing Susi back shot through her mind. But it was only the Inspector and the Sergeant, evidently returned in time for the promised phone call from the kidnappers . . .

The heat had drained away from the day now, moths flew against the window, a bat swooped low from the depths of the sweetly perfumed wisteria which wound about the window frame. At any other time she would have drunk in the beauty, taken a deep joy in the peace and tranquility which was all about her ... But now all she could think about was the impending phone call and all it implied.

She crossed the room and opened the door. Below there were raised voices, footsteps in the hall. Slowly she started down the stairs. It seemed as if her whole life up to this moment was culminating in the mechanics of walking from one step to another of the deep carpeted stairs, her hand slid down the polished wood of the banister. She had an acute awareness, a crystalline vision of every detail about her ...

The big grandfather clock in the hall started to chime the hour. For an eternity ... then as the last stroke died away, she quickly crossed the hall and went into the library where David and the two policemen waited ... The engineers stood by the tape recorder, their backs to her. It was like a still from a film ... then as she hesitated in the doorway, four pairs of eyes turned

71

towards her . . . she put out her hand in an involuntary gesture, like a sleepwalker.

Instinctively David came towards her, leading her to the sofa.

'They're late aren't they?' she asked.

He smiled. 'I think the clock may be a little fast. If they call from a public box, which I expect they will, they may have to wait, there could be a delay for any number of reasons . . .'

In the silence the beating of her heart was deafening.

Then suddenly the quiet was ripped apart . . . there was a crash in the hall as something heavy slithered across the polished boards, the tinkle of glass . . . running footsteps on the gravel . . . like lightning the Sergeant leapt through the french windows and raced along the terrace to the drive in front of the house. The Inspector with equal speed went through the door into the hall, shouting as he went to David and Alison. 'Stay where you are, it may be a trick, a bomb, anything . . .'

Alison needed no bidding, she sat where she was as if paralysed, unable to move with the shock of the crash when she had been straining for the sound of the phone bell . . .

David stood where he had half started after the Inspector, near the door . . .

The Sergeant was the first to return, panting as he said: 'Lost him . . . they had a car . . . couldn't even get the number . . . had too much of a start . . . sounded like a sports job . . . why the hell didn't we think to leave a patrol car at the bottom of the drive . . . '

As he spoke, the Inspector came in from the hall, a small black box in his hand . . .

'What on earth . . . ?' David began.

The Inspector gave a shrug of his shoulders . . . 'A cassette,' he said slowly, 'the modern version of the brick with a message tied to it . . . '

Alison watched him as he went over to the machine, clicked the cassette into the slot and pushed down the button . . .

For a moment the only sound that broke the silence was a crackling of surface noise — then a sharp intake of breath — and the flute-like sound of a child's voice, as she said:

'Hullo, Mummy — Mummy this is me — Susi . . . '

5

At the sound of Susi's voice Alison leapt to her feet, an exclamation half of surprise, half of anguish escaping her lips.

'Susi!'

The name exploded from her as she stretched out her hands, reaching in a gesture of longing and impatience. Then she sank back on the sofa, realising it was simply a recording — dropping her head on her hands as the tape went relentlessly on, a harsh voice now replacing Susi's . . .

'That fooled you stupid fuzz didn't it? So bloody sure of yourselves. Well don't be because we're one jump ahead all the time. There's been a bit of a foul up — we don't have the kid we intended, the Beresford kid. The one we're holding's called Susi, so she tells us. Seems from what she says her ma works for you, Beresford — Alison Ross. But don't get excited — it don't make no difference to us whose brat it is. If her ma wants to see her again someone's going to have to deliver the lollie. We're going to take a break to think it over. It might just change things. So I'll be in touch tomorrow. Give you twenty-four hours to think it over Beresford, and think careful mate, we mean business with this snatch. It's just your good luck it isn't your kid, but if you want this one to stay fit and well the conditions are just the same, see? So don't try any funny business with the fuzz. Just do as you're told. If I was you I'd call the nosy bleeders off anyway, they don't do no good. Till tomorrow about 11 then.'

Now only the hum of the machine filled the silent room.

The Inspector leaned forward and pressed the re-wind button, turning to Alison.

'Must be television addicts — no

doubt they've seen this method used . . . '

She still sat with her face hidden in her hands. Hearing Susi's voice so vividly that she might have been in the room, had filled her with fresh misery and anguish.

'Now Mr. Beresford, Mrs. Ross, I'll just play it again in case either of you can recognise anything about the voice . . . '

It had been the kind of nondescript voice you heard every day — no regional accent, nothing. Flat, monotonous, toneless . . .

'Of course,' he went on, 'he was probably using the prescribed method of speaking through a piece of cloth . . . ' As he mumbled on a sob escaped Alison.

Quickly David went to where she sat, putting his arm round her. It was as if his touch realeased something — some tension which had been holding her together, she crumpled up against him. His whole attitude was one of protecting her as he looked up at the Inspector.

'It won't be necessary now, it will

have to wait. Mrs. Ross is simply in no condition to be harrassed — there's nothing that can't wait until later.' He knew she was near breaking point and that to hear Susi's voice again would simply be intolerable.

The Inspector gave him a stony look and said reluctantly, 'Very well, sir, but I'm afraid it will only be with her co-operation — and yours of course — that we can proceed as quickly as we would like.'

He snapped the cassette from the machine and replaced it in its plastic holder, slipping it into his pocket.

'I'll take this back to the station, the experts will want to work on it.'

He picked up his hat and went towards the door, signalling to Sergeant Mitchell to follow him. At the door he turned.

'Incidentally, as is usual, we shall play along with the villains as far as possible. The general idea is to become as unobstrusive as we can, our object of course is always to obtain the return of the hostage — our primary concern. Catching the kidnappers can only be attempted once that is achieved . . . naturally we hope to accomplish both . . . '

He smiled bleakly in Alison's direction — a smile which didn't reach his eyes.

It made no difference to her as her face was buried in the comfort of David's broad shoulder. It all seemed hopeless, like trying to swim upstream against an overwhelming current.

'One more thing,' the Inspector said, 'I should be obliged if you would make sure you do not speak to the press or anyone else involved with any of the media. From bitter experience we have found it is better to persuade them to hold this kind of story — in the past there have been 'leaks,' such an occurrence can only jeopardise the ultimate success of the enterprise.'

Neither David nor Alison replied. As far as she was concerned she didn't care who knew or who didn't. All she wanted was Susi, the feel of her arms round her neck, the softness of her skin.

David held her close. There was a sweet, fresh perfume about her rather like a small child — and yet she had an air of maturity, of independence. He didn't want to intrude on her grief, and yet to his own surprise he found he wanted her to know he cared — deeply.

Was it only because he knew how he would have felt if it had been Jo-Anne? Or even perhaps Sarah herself the kidnappers had taken — or was it something else, something more. A deep tenderness at least . . . of that he was certain.

She stirred, lifting her head, looking at him from tear filled eyes that somehow reminded him of the deep blue flowers he had once seen as a child, growing in a stream . . .

'Isn't there anything . . . anything at all we can do?' Her voice was scarcely above a whisper.

'I know it seems impossible to you,' he said slowly, 'but you are going to have to try and sleep. There are twenty-four hours to be lived through before we hear anything more — and for Susi's sake, as well as yours, you have to stay as fresh and rested as you can.'

Her head jerked up against his chin. 'You don't mean the police are just going to sit and do nothing till they hear from them again?' She looked towards the tape machine which stood by the telephone, at the empty cassette player David had borrowed from Sarah to listen to the recording . . .

'No, I'm sure they will be doing everything they can, following up any tiny shred of evidence — but to be fair at the moment there isn't much to go on — just the cassette and what we have told them. We do have to be patient, to trust them . . .'

As he spoke the young Sergeant, who had been adjusting the plug which led from the wall to the recording machine — playing for time after his superior had left the room — turned round and said, 'Mrs. Ross, please believe me, we will do everything humanly possible . . . '

She glanced at him in surprise, unaware he was still in the room.

'At the moment,' he went on, smiling down at her, 'it is rather like looking for the proverbial needle in the haystack — with money as the motive in a kidnapping it really makes things even more tricky than usual. There are so many amateur villains who read about a snatch and think it's easy money. Usually the more professional ones who do it for political reasons, or some other motive and are probably already on our files — are easier to trace. At least in their cases we have some kind of lead . . . ' he hesitated, 'but if it is of any comfort, and these are amateurs, which I very much suspect, being confused now that their plan has misfired, it is more than likely they'll be only too glad to return your little girl unharmed and quickly . . . ' He paused, again.

David got to his feet with a little gesture of impatience. He resented the young man for some reason — a young man about Alison's own age — good looking too. He supposed he meant well, rather better than the Inspector, whom he didn't like at all — perhaps he was being unreasonable, but he said shortly,

'Thank you Sergeant, I think it would be best if Mrs. Ross was allowed to rest now.'

Mitchell raised a quizzical eyebrow at him, a smile touching his lips. He recognised jealousy when he saw it, and there was no denying, in spite of her unhappiness, Alison Ross was an outstandingly beautiful girl . . . maybe when all this was over . . . he thought of his own empty house now his wife, Chris, had gone — empty except for a small boy . . . he nodded . . .

'I agree, and I know it's useless to say 'Don't worry', of course you will, but you're going to be much more help to us and Susi if you do as Mr. Beresford suggests, and get some rest.

He leant forward and patted her

shoulder. She looked up at him gratefully giving him a watery smile. 'I will try to be sensible, and thank you Sergeant.' He seemed more of a human being than the rather impersonal Inspector . . .

David had gone over and opened the door with ill concealed impatience, holding it open, his hand on the knob.

'Then the sooner you leave us, the better — the more quickly she will be able to rest,' he said with an edge to his voice . . .

As the front door closed, there was the sound of another car drawing up. For a moment a ridiculous little flame of hope spurted up inside Alison, but David said quickly.

'It's Doctor Irvine, I asked him to come along just to have a look at you . . . '

She opened her mouth to protest, but the doctor came into the room, a bag in one hand, his stethoscope swinging from the other.

'Hullo David, came as soon as I

could. Tricky baby case — twins . . . but I've left Jeff to cope, boy must win his spurs . . . thought you sounded a bit put out . . . some kind of trouble is there?' He glanced at Alison with interest.

'This is Mrs. Ross — Alison Ross. She works at Beresfords . . . ' Alison got up now, looking from one man to the other.

'It's quite ridiculous, I don't need a doctor. There's nothing wrong with me . . . '

David nodded, 'I know, and I intend to keep things that way, and I thought a sleeping pill perhaps, something to help you relax . . . '

He explained briefly to the doctor what had happened. He clicked open his bag, 'Very wise.' He sorted among the contents as David told him the details of the kidnapping.

Once more Alison felt near to tears, but this time the cause was different, for she couldn't remember when last anyone had been genuinely concerned for her well being, and somehow it did seem David really meant it . . . the doctor too was kind. He asked her one or two questions and then gave her a small bottle of pills.

'Just a couple with some warm milk, they'll help you sleep, my dear.' He patted her hand as she took the bottle from him. After a few more words with David he said his goodbyes and going towards the door said, 'I'll see myself out thanks David, after all I know this place nearly as well as you do!'

Mrs. Finlay bustled into the room with a tray of warm milk and biscuits. David took it from her. 'Thank you, I'll see Mrs. Ross upstairs, you go on to bed.'

'If you're sure sir.' She nodded at Alison 'I hope you get some sleep, Miss . . . '

Alison followed David up the wide stairs, feeling rather like a small child. He put the tray down on the bedside table and switched on the shaded light. It made a small soft pool of brightness, throwing the rest of the room into shadowed relief. But now suddenly everything whirled round like a carousel, she put out her hand with a little moan of fear, David swung round just in time to catch her ... lifting her gently in his arms, he carried her across to the bed. He could feel the bones through the soft flesh. It reminded him of the delicate frame of a bird he had picked up when it had fallen, exhausted, from some electric wires — a swallow newly arrived from Africa ... she was something like a bird, he thought as he stood holding her, looking down at the pale face, the delicate blue veins on her closed lids, the long sweep of silky lashes on the curve of her cheek.

She didn't look much more than a child herself, vulnerable, needing protection, he felt a flood of compassion ... was it compassion or something more. It certainly wasn't any fatherly feeling he had for her, not as he would have done had it been Sarah in his arms — more a rush of deep emotion. Protective, primitive almost — perhaps more than that — the normal feelings of a man in his prime for a beautiful young woman. Suddenly some lines from Yeats' poem, 'The Pity of Love', flashed into his mind and he murmured the words as he looked down at her — 'A pity beyond all telling is hid in the heart of love . . . '

She stirred and opened her eyes, struggling to be free . . . gently he laid her on the bed, then bent down and pulled off her shoes. She tried to sit up, to protest . . .

'Please — I'm so sorry I passed out. I'll be all right now, quite all right . . .' she tried to smile. 'So stupid, I don't ever remember doing that before . . . '

With an instinctive gesture he smoothed back the tumbled fair hair, feeling a renewed thrill as he touched its silky softness — like corn gold — he thought briefly . . . no, richer than that, a fresh peeled chestnut . . . I'm getting senile, he pulled himself up abruptly — maundering on like a lovesick schoolboy or a frustrated old man . . . and God knows I'm neither.

He shook his head slowly. 'Now look, just drink up the milk and take a couple of the pills, they're quite harmless, I've had them myself before now.'

She looked up at him from those blue waterweed eyes . . .

He turned away quickly, rejecting the sudden suffocating desire he had to kiss her on the lips, to caress her — make love to her even . . .

She drew herself up and leaned against the soft pillows, looking ruefully at the dress Sarah had lent her. Now alas it too was almost as crumpled as the one she had taken off earlier.

'I must hang up this dress, it's Sarah's . . . '

He turned round again with a little gesture of impatience, 'Good heavens, I shouldn't worry about that, she's got cupboards full . . . ' he hesitated, 'would you like me to call Mrs. Finlay to give you a hand?'

She swung her feet to the ground, 'No, I'm perfectly all right now — it was stupid of me to pass out like that . . . I think it was partly the shock of that cassette — the way it came through the glass . . . and Susi . . . ' her voice quavered uncertainly.

He nodded, 'Yes, and that was exactly what it was meant to do, shock us, we were all strung up and waiting for a phone call.' He opened the door, 'Now try and get some sleep, and don't come down for breakfast, it's a rather movable feast anyway. Mrs. Finlay will bring you something on a tray. Good night . . . '

Before she could open her mouth to protest at the thought of breakfast in bed, he had opened the door and gone.

Out on the landing he found he was trembling, the feel of that soft supple body in his arms had filled him with desires and longings he had thought were all in the past. With shaking fingers he took out a cigarette and lighted it, drawing in long breaths of the comforting smoke . . .

Alison slid off the bed and undressed, putting on the blue cotton pyjamas she'd brought from the flat. They looked even more faded and shabby in the luxurious surroundings. But she was past caring . . .

She went over to the window and drew back the heavy curtains, pushing open the french windows which led on to a small balcony above the terrace. As she stepped out into the cool night air she could hear the sweet sound of a fountain somewhere splashing into a basin, above her the upturned bowl of night was jet velvet, hung with millions of stars. She could pick out the Great Bear . . . how often she and Susi had looked at it together, and the child had lifted up Huggy Bear saying 'There's one of your relations, Huggy,' and then turned to her mother saying solemnly, 'do you think that's where all the bears go when they die, Mum? like the dogs go to the Dog Star?'

And Alison had put her arm round her and smiled, saying, 'I shouldn't be at all surprised, love . . . '

Remembering now, the tears started to flow again as she wondered where Susi was, and if she could see the stars too, and what a small girl might suffer in the hands of unscrupulous men . . . it seemed almost too much to endure herself — the anguish and pain that filled her heart, and for a moment she wished she could feel the warm arms of David, strong, supporting her, and hear the gentleness in his voice as he tried to comfort her . . .

She climbed into the luxurious bed, finished the milk and swallowed the pills — mostly because David had asked her to . . .

She switched off the light and the great oblong shape of the window sprang into opalescence. Far away she could hear the hum of the traffic on the by-pass. The house itself seemed to have settled down, the only sound,

some soft music probably from a radio
. . . an owl hooted nearby, a dog barked
. . . she closed her eyes and tried to
relax . . . but all the time Susi's face
danced in front of her, and her mind
recalled in every detail the day that lay
behind her, of all she and Susi had
talked about . . . at breakfast the child
had said, 'Hope the day'll be better
than yesterday, Mum . . . ' almost now
as if it had been some terrible
foreboding . . . but then she had smiled
and said 'What was so awful about
yesterday?'

'Well, that Stevie, the one with the
hamster, he found a tiny frog in the
garden and put it on the table at lunch,
it was awful. Miss Ransome told him to
take it back to its mother, it was too
little to leave her, you see . . . '

Alison choked on the memory — like
the little frog which Susi didn't want
hurt, she too was too little to leave her
mother . . .

What monsters could have done such
a thing to a small girl who had never

harmed anyone — who hadn't even started to live her life. The terrible things she had read in the papers in the past started to unwind themselves through her mind . . .

She stared into the darkness. She felt helpless, trapped, like a caged animal behind iron bars . . . it was so hopeless, how could she give the police any help for whoever the kidnappers were it was against David they held a grudge, not her, he was the one who should have to identify them . . .

For a moment she felt a little spurt of resentment against him. It was unfair that it had been his grandchild they had meant to take, he who had everything — and yet she who had so little had been the one who had been the victim, had all she lived for taken from her.

As quickly as the thought had risen, she dismissed it. It could hardly be said to be his fault, and he was doing all he could to help her, of that she was certain.

How odd it was that she had worked

in the firm for so long, and yet it had been tragedy that had brought them together . . .

She turned over on her side. She guessed he must be in his late forties, Sarah was about her own age . . . he didn't look that old . . . her lids felt heavy as though they had weights on them . . . it was as though she were falling, falling . . . down into deep darkness . . . it wasn't an unpleasant feeling, more like floating . . . For a moment she forgot everything but the feeling of lightness — and she remembered the look in David's eyes as he'd watched her while the doctor talked to her . . . as if he really did care . . .

6

The soft knock on the door roused her.

She jerked bolt upright in the bed, thinking she'd overslept and it was Susi waking her . . . then as she saw the sun streaming through the open french windows, reflecting all the colours of the rainbow from the cut glass jars and bottles on the dressing table — with a sinking heart she remembered . . . Like a huge dark cloud, yesterday came back . . .

She glanced at the breakfast tray Mrs. Finlay put on the side table. Beautiful eggshell thin china, polished silver, even a red rose in a tiny glass holder — for a brief moment she wondered if that had been David's idea to try and comfort her as she woke . . . The coffee smelt wonderful . . . but she turned her head away . . .

'I'm sorry, when you've been to all

that trouble, but I coudn't possibly eat anything . . . maybe it's the sleeping pills, I feel so heavy and my mouth's dry . . . ' her voice tailed off.

The woman bustled round the room, twitching the curtains, pushing the windows a little further open so that dusty sunlight flooded into the room. Alison could hear the fluting tones of a child's voice, the splash of water as someone dived into the pool — and laughter — it only made her misery more acute, more difficult to bear, and suddenly she longed for David again as she had before she fell asleep. He was her sheet anchor, all she had to cling to.

'What on earth is the time?' she picked up her watch from the table, and realised she'd forgotten to wind it.

'Now Miss, Mr. Beresford said you were to stay in bed as long as you liked. 'Tis only half past nine, and he won't be going to the office today, he said to tell you . . . '

'Half past nine!' Alison broke in, 'I must have been asleep for hours

. . . how could I . . . '

She pushed the hair back from her face. Already heat filled the room, bringing the promise of yet another stifling day. Her heart cried out, 'Oh Susi, my little love, where are you, and how are you this bright morning . . . if only I knew you were all right . . . that they hadn't hurt you . . . '

Mrs. Finlay poured the coffee, adding cream and sugar. 'Now come on, lovey drink this, then maybe you'll feel like tackling the egg, 'tis fresh as the morning itself. From our own hens, Mr. Beresford's very particular Miss Jo-Anne should have only the best . . . ' She cut herself short as she caught sight of the expression on Alison's face, realising too late she'd been tactless to mention the child, she went on quickly 'Miss Sarah said to ask if there's anything you want in the way of clothes, she thought you might like a swim later, said to tell you she's got a spare bikini . . . ' she sniffed, 'got a whole box full I shouldn't wonder . . . '

Alison sipped the coffee. It was as good as its fragrance had promised, not much like the instant brew she was used to, she thought wryly . . . Somehow the long day which stretched ahead, had to be lived through . . . the phone call — if it was a phone call this time — wasn't due till 11 o'clock that night. Why did they have to wait so long? Simply to prolong the agony she supposed, squeeze the last drop of pain from everyone concerned so they would pay up . . . suddenly, for the first time, she thought about the money, no one had said how much the sum would be . . . thousands of pounds perhaps . . . if it hadn't been so ghastly, it would have been laughable that anyone should ask her for money — she had nothing but her salary. She supposed she could borrow some from David . . . but she'd never be able to pay it back, she couldn't even afford a mortgage on a house. Although in a way he had assumed responsibility, she could hardly expect him to provide ransom money for a child he'd never even seen, who after all, meant nothing to him . . .

She tried to eat a piece of the melba toast, but it stuck in her throat . . . The dress Sarah had leant her hung where she had left it, somehow mocking in its expensive simplicity — her own hung, freshly washed and pressed, beside it . . . how smoothly life ran with money . . . it didn't mean everything she knew — money — but she wasn't stupid enough to despise it, it could oil the wheels of living — and now perhaps even bring back Susi . . .

She slipped out of bed and going over to the long mirror on the wall, gazed at her reflection. Hollow cheeks, pale skin, huge eyes, the pupils dilated — enlarged she supposed by the sleeping pills. She still felt only half awake, but whether that was the drugs or the experiences of yesterday she didn't know, or really care . . .

She had a shower, brushed out her hair and coiled it on top of her head to keep it off her neck. She didn't often wear it that way, somehow it made her look severe — and Johnnie had never liked it . . . funny how seldom she thought of him now — it was somehow as if he'd never been, except for Susi . . .

Slowly she went down the stairs and out of the open glass doors on to the patio that surrounded the swimming pool. She didn't feel like being alone, on the other hand she didn't feel like making small talk with anyone . . . but somehow the very fact of the hours of the day had to be lived through.

Sarah was reclining on a shaded seat, slowly swinging backward and forwards, Brian, her husband, was in the pool, teaching Jo-Anne to swim, they splashed and laughed, the small girl screaming with delight as her father lifted her up and then dropped her back in the water, her bright orange inflated armlets holding her on the surface.

Alison stood for a moment, feeling forlorn, outside the circle of happiness and so alone . . . suddenly there was a touch on her arm and she swung round. David stood with a glass of orange juice in his hand, the ice clinking against the sides. He had on a blue silk shirt and navy slacks, beautifully cut, and so casual she knew they must have cost the earth. She couldn't see the expression in his eyes behind the sunglasses, but his mouth was gentle as he said, 'I hope you got some sleep and that you feel a little rested at least.'

The intense heat from the tiles of the patio already shimmered like an oven, he took her arm and drew her to a seat under one of the brightly coloured umbrellas, then he held out the glass of orange juice, giving a lopsided smile. 'Have a sip of this, at least it gives an illusion of coolness, and then perhaps later on you'd like a swim.'

She felt a sudden and totally unreasonable annoyance, that the life of the people in this house could apparently go on as normal while her whole world had collapsed around her, and it seemed at the moment as though nothing were being done. She shook her head, 'No thanks,' she said shortly.

He gave her a quick look, then taking off the sun glasses, passed them to her.

'Look, wear these, the glare from the tiles and the water is very trying.'

She put them on and the tinted glass brought a measure of relief. She knew now why so many people these days wore dark glasses, they were a kind of barrier against the world, a means of hiding one's feelings, from reality even — a symbol of modern living and the retreat from the gaze of the world outside.

'The Inspector called earlier on, but I wouldn't have you disturbed,' David said quietly.

She looked up quickly. 'Did he say anything — I mean is there any news, anything at all?'

He shook his head reluctantly. 'I'm afraid not. It's no good expecting any until tonight, so between us we have to get through the day as best we can.'

Now he smiled at her and she could see his eyes, tender, compassionate, as though she were a small, bruised child.

'Waiting, trying to be patient, this is the worst part of all,' he hesitated, watching Sarah who was shouting at Jo-Anne, who had bounced out of the pool like a playful puppy, and run to her mother as Brian chased her. Sarah was annoyed because she had made the swing and her sundress damp . . .

For a moment Alison closed her eyes thinking 'You wouldn't shout at her if you knew how precious they can suddenly become.' She was glad she'd never shouted at Susi — oh she'd been cross with her sometimes of course — but she hoped never without justification . . .

She opened her eyes again. Brian stood with his hands on his hips, waiting for his wife's tirade to cease . . . as if he sensed her feelings, David stood up and took Alison's hand, drawing her to her feet.

'Come inside for a bit, the sun is

really getting a bit too much, it's beautifully cool in the drawing room.'

Cream venetian blinds covered the windows, making a kind of twilight with bars of sunshine, motes of dust floating in them, the heavy perfume of the roses in the beds outside, filled the room.

She became aware of the portrait which hung over the stone fireplace. She hadn't noticed it last night.

She stood for a moment looking at it. She felt, rather than heard, him come up behind her.

'That was my wife, Joy,' he said softly, 'her name well chosen.'

She turned and looked at him, seeing his eyes were bright with unshed tears. He gave a wry smile, 'I know it's ridiculous, after all these years, she died when Sarah was born. I'm not usually given to emotional scenes, and I don't talk about Joy to anyone, but I think somehow you understand.'

She turned back again to the portrait, looking at this woman whose memory could still make a grown man cry, and warmed to him, understanding. From the painting she didn't look especially beautiful, but the artist had caught a kind of wistfulness, a humour and gentleness of expression which were far deeper than beauty.

'I should like to have known her,' she said softly, 'she was lucky at least that she knew what real love was, even if only for a short time.' Her voice had a poignancy.

'It is something not granted to all of us,' he said slowly.

She looked at him now and thought, 'I've got to tell him, I've got to put the record straight.'

'I'm not married,' she said shortly, 'I made a mistake with the wrong man . . . '

For a moment he didn't answer, then he put out his hands and drew her into the circle of his arms.

'I know, my dear . . . '

'But how . . . ?' she asked, surprise in her voice . . .

'Quite simply. I got your file from

personnel, I didn't want to have to ask you questions about your private life — nor the police — not to embarrass you in front of other people.'

For a moment she was taken aback — amazed at the depth of his sensitivity. And now there was something about the way he spoke, the way he looked at her that loosened the floodgate of misery, not just the misery she was living through at the moment, the loss of Susi — but the misery of the constant battle her life seemed to be, the deep scars of sorrow that were etched in her heart — and so she told him . . .

As she spoke quietly into the well of silence, the sounds from outside came muted into the shadowed room where they sat . . . the laughter of the child the shouts of Brian, the distant hum of traffic, all unreal compared with the stark facts she told him . . .

'I won't bore you with all the details of the difficulties, it hasn't been easy managing and I was terribly lonely at first — but Susi became everything to me, made it all worthwhile,' her voice broke as she uttered the last words, and she started to sob uncontrollably.

He gathered her close to him, feeling an overwhelming tenderness and an undeniable passionate longing.

It was all so very different from what he had imagined when he first read the file and saw that she was an unmarried mother . . . he'd been inclined to sit in judgment, now he realised how wrong he had been. This girl had not only an innate freshness, a kind of purity, but immense courage . . . in spite of which he knew she needed him and the knowledge filled him with warmth, and a kind of excited anticipation . . .

'I'm sorry,' she murmured against the soft silk of his shirt, 'I never cry — never . . . '

He could believe it. She was not the type who felt the world owed her a living, who didn't even seem to envy Sarah who had everything money could buy, who was sheltered and cushioned by love from the harshness of the outside world.

No, this girl had nothing, no one ... she's far too thin, he thought inconsequently as he held her ... but whatever happened he determined he would protect her as much as he could, be her natural comforter, solid, dependable — a trifle dull perhaps — but always there — good old David ...

He drew immense comfort from the thought ...

7

The longest day Alison ever remembered drew slowly towards its close. The shadows from the giant elms round the lawn lengthened, and the evening star hung huge and bright in the incandescent sky.

Sarah and Brian, both immaculate in evening dress, left for a dance in a cloud of French perfume, Jo-Anne had been somewhat reluctantly read to sleep and Mrs. Finlay had the evening off . . .

Now Alison stood looking out at the twilit garden, moths fluttered round the evening primroses, she could smell the heady perfume of the tobacco plant, somewhere an owl hooted — 'old hooty owls' Susi called them . . . Susi . . . would she be back with her tomorrow by this time? She gave an involuntary sound, half moan, half sigh, and David came up behind her . . .

'Drink this, it may help . . . '

She turned round . . . 'I . . . ' she hesitated, not wanting once more to appear ungrateful, he'd been so kind and patient.

He grinned, 'Boss's orders!'

Her fingers closed round the heavy crystal goblet, and the brandy caught the rays of the dying sun.

'I don't know about you,' he went on, 'but I'm starving. I told Mrs. Finlay not to bother with any food, I guessed you might not feel like a sit-down meal in the dining room,' he paused, 'would it be asking too much to get you to make us something light — an omelette and salad perhaps?' He glanced at his watch, 'there's still an hour before they're due to ring.'

She had shied away from the thought, remembering with reluctant vividness the last time they had promised. Now they had had twenty-four hours to think about it, to mull over what they were going to do under the changed circumstances. Would it have altered their plan? Would it mean Susi was in more danger or less? Suddenly she realised he was waiting for her reply. She put the untouched glass down on the table near the tape recorder.

'Of course, I'd be only too pleased.' Actually she'd never felt less like cooking an omelette in her life, but it would be churlish to refuse. He took her arm and led her through the hall, pushing open the green baize door which swished quietly behind them.

It was the kind of kitchen she had seen with envy in glossie magazines, she caught her breath as she gazed round at the shining copper pans on the walls, the hot plates, the cupboards and drawers which swung open at a finger tip touch, there were enough electric gadgets to delight any cook's heart.

David stood quietly watching her face, 'Mrs. Finlay looks after us very well, and it suits Sarah to let her do the cooking for them as well. There's a service lift to their flat,' he went over and showed Alison how it worked and the hot plate built in to keep everything sizzling with heat until it arrived in Sarah's kitchen.

Alison smiled tremulously, 'I feel a bit overawed, I haven't even used an electric mixer in my life — but if you'll show me where everything is I'll see what I can do.'

As she broke the brown eggs with their rich yolks — so different from the pale supermarket brand — and chopped fresh herbs David brought from the garden — to her surprise she found that she was hungry, and the smell of the butter bubbling and browning in the thick pan teased her taste buds.

David tossed salad in a wooden bowl and said smiling, 'I can't remember when I had such fun. I've eaten alone for so long in that rather overpowering dining room, I'd almost forgotten how good simple food tastes — not that I've anything against Mrs. F's cooking, it's just lack of company . . . it's nice and homely in the kitchen like this . . . '

The coffee bubbled in the percolator, filling the room with the rich smell of fresh ground beans. He sniffed appreciatively, 'Trouble is, like many things in life, the anticipation of coffee is so often much better than the realisation, but this time it isn't going to be, we'll have cream and forget all the dietician's advice,' he looked at her slim waist and hips, then added, 'not that you need worry.'

She felt the warm colour rising in her face, she couldn't remember the last time any man had remarked on her appearance . . .

David cut thin bread and butter, and Alison slid the light, fluffy omelettes on to the warm plates.

'Mm, makes my mouth water, drool in fact,' he said looking at their crisp brown edges 'I can see you are one of those rare people who are experts in making omelettes . . . '

They sat in companionable silence, appreciating the food, the coffee was excellent and he fetched her brandy glass from the other room, filling one for himself, and sipping it with the coffee, pouring the thick rich cream on its surface over the back with a spoon.

As she watched him she said, 'Susi'd like to see you do that . . . ' . . . then wished she hadn't spoken her name . . . and suddenly she knew she had to ask him, to broach the subject of money which had been niggling at the back of her mind since the first message had arrived from the kidnappers. She said abruptly, her tone sharpened by anxiety . . .

'What are we . . . I mean what can I do about the money they're going to want for Susi . . . I have nothing but my salary . . . '

For a moment he didn't speak, twirling the stem of his brandy glass, then he put it down and took one of her hands in both his, turning it over and gently stroking the palm.

'My dear child, all that is taken care of, I have already been to the bank, the manager is an old friend, and I've withdrawn what I consider to be adequate — at least what the Inspector seems to think they will ask . . . '

She looked up at him fearfully. 'Is there some kind of standard amount then, a fixed price . . . ?'

He smiled briefly, his eyes sliding away from hers. 'Not exactly, but it seems pretty obvious this is the work of amateurs, who have probably lost their nerve now on finding they've made a proper nonsense of the whole job and will be glad to settle for a reasonable sum, so as neither to lose face nor cause too many difficulties — the Inspector is of the opinion they will simply ask for an amount which they would think a man in my position could afford . . . '

She didn't answer, wondering what kind of money was really involved. To her five hundred pounds was like a king's ransom — she had no idea what David or the Inspector would think of as adequate.

As if he were reading her mind, he

said softly 'Don't worry, I've got £20,000 locked in my wall safe — I don't think there's much doubt that should cover it.'

She gasped 'But I'll never be able to repay that amount!'

'Of course not, and why should you? It's me they're after, not you. That it was your Susi and not my Jo-Anne that was snatched is incidental — the basic demand is still from me.'

He got to his feet, 'Come along, I'll show you to set your mind at rest.'

She followed him back into the sitting room, he switched on a standard lamp which threw a little pool of golden light in the surrounding twilight of the summer evening. Going over to a picture that hung above the bureau, he removed it and revealed a wall safe. She heard the clicks as he turned the combination. Then he opened the door and took out a small case, snapping open the lid. Inside were bundles of notes, all used. He smiled at her, 'They always ask for used ones, can't think why, the bank has the numbers of these anyway . . . '

As he spoke a car drew up outside and the Inspector and Sergeant came from the terrace through the french windows.

'Good evening Mrs. Ross, Mr. Beresford.' The Inspector nodded briefly at them, the Sergeant however gave Alison a warm smile and a thumbs up sign, grinning like a small boy as he did so. The Inspector went over to the tape recorder and started to go through the routine of checking it to make sure it was in working order.

'A drink, Inspector?' David asked.

The man shook his head. 'No thank you, sir, never on duty . . . ' He probably didn't mean it, but he looked and sounded smug.

'Your alcohol intake must be pretty small then,' David said drily, there was something about this man that got under his skin. The Inspector made no comment, simply telling the Sergeant to test the equipment. As he did so, the phone rang. Alison's heart seemed to stop for a moment — and then, without really knowing what she did, as if motivated by some unseen power, she snatched up the instrument, crying . . . 'Susi! Susi! I want to speak to my child . . . please please, just for a moment . . . that's all I ask . . . '

Before there could be any reply from the caller, David took the phone from her, firmly but deliberately, meanwhile the Inspector had thrown out his hand as if he were going to knock it from her grasp, then they stood as if paralysed, watching David, his eyes half closed as he concentrated on the voice from the other end. The recording machine spools were the only things that moved in the room with a tiny hiss . . . the Inspector had now snatched up the other phone which had been temporarily installed to give directions to headquarters to try and trace the call, as David slowly, and deliberately made the caller repeat his message . . . then there was a click as he rang off. Alison watched him replace the receiver, her hands clasped so that the knuckles showed white.

'What did they say, is Susi all right? When will they send her back? I'm sorry, I know I shouldn't have done that . . . '

He put his arm round her. 'You shall hear the whole thing on the tape.' He turned now to the Inspector who was re-winding it. 'I kept them talking as long as possible — I hope it was of some use.'

The Inspector gave a brief nod 'Thank you, sir. They are trying to trace the call, sure to be a public box so I don't hold out much hope in that direction . . . '

David broke in now, speaking softly, almost as if to himself, 'There was something — I'll be more certain when I hear the run back — but in the part where you hear Susi's voice — there's a different man's voice, brief — but I'm sure I recognised it . . . '

The Sergeant glanced up from the

machine, his face suddenly and sharply aware. 'Someone you know sir? Someone from your factory?'

David nodded, 'Could be. The trouble is the name is on the edge of my memory,' he tapped his forehead impatiently, 'up here in the computer. It may take a little time for the wheels to turn . . . '

The Sergeant switched on the machine and the same voice as they had heard on the cassette said, 'We shall want 10,000 quid in old notes, bring them to the fun fair at Dawlish Warren, in a sports bag with Adidas on the side in white letters — a black bag, it must be black and new. Put it down by the shooting gallery — you can't miss it . . . ' the voice hesitated a moment and then became indistinct as the speaker obviously turned his head away from the mike and said, 'Hi, you, kid . . . what's that bear of yours called?' It was then they heard Susi's childish treble — 'Huggy Bear of course, silly, I told you already . . . ' It was then the other man's voice said,

'Shut up, kid . . . '

Alison gave a little cry as she heard Susi, but David held up his hand, 'Could we have that bit again, where the other man breaks in . . . '

He sat with his hands holding his bowed head as the sergeant played the words over and over . . .

Then suddenly he leapt to his feet. 'I've got it! It's Sid Honeysett. He used to drive for me, then I promoted him to stores foreman — but there were a series of thefts, goods that kept disappearing, and in the end it was all traced to him . . . ' He glanced at the Inspector looking a bit sheepish, 'I know it was wrong, this whole thing proves it now, but I didn't report it to you chaps. I took the law into my own hands, didn't want him in more trouble, and put him back on driving. I suppose he felt resentful and bitter, wanted to get his own back, and planned the snatch . . . '

'And you have his address, Mr. Beresford?'

David shook his head, 'I doubt it, he left some time ago and I believe went up north. But I suppose he came back, possibly just to do this job. Probably he drove the lorry into the quarry, banking on the fact that he wouldn't be noticed among the general confusion, and he must have picked Susi up in the lane . . . '

Alison grabbed his arm 'What kind of person is he? Would he hurt Susi?'

He shook his head, 'No, I think that's one thing we can be sure of,' he hesitated, 'the kind perhaps who bears a grudge, thinks the world owes him a living — in fact now I come to think about it, his wife left him and took their little girl with her — about Susi's age. He worshipped her — the child — so I can't imagine him hurting any young thing . . . '

She sank down on the sofa, covering her face with her hands.

'Well at least we do have a lead now sir,' the Inspector said 'I think we had better hear the rest of the tape . . . '

Briefly it said that early the next morning David was to leave the money as directed, in due course, if the instructions were followed in detail Susi would be returned . . . how was not divulged. But if there was any slip up or interference by the fuzz, they would promise nothing . . . David was to take the train and get off at the small station, nothing much more than a halt which served the beach and fun fair, crowded with holiday-makers at this time of year . . .

So now at last there was activity. Alison begged to be allowed to go with David, even if she kept out of sight — but both he and the C.I.D. men were adamant, 'If we deviate by one degree from their instructions we are asking for trouble, Mrs. Ross. And it is certain Susi won't be with whoever collects the money, so no useful purpose would be served. If you wait here we'll leave a policewoman with you if you wish, but we must do exactly as they say . . . ' He was about to add, 'It's our only hope . . . ' but thought better of it.

David did take Alison into town with him however to buy the bag, and then back at the house together they counted out the notes. It seemed incredible to her, handling enough money to have kept her and Susi for the rest of their lives — in the way they were accustomed to live anyway — and yet it was only money, pieces of paper, and Susi was all she had, something no money could buy, and yet now, all that could bring her safely back.

David watched her, guessing at some of her thoughts. 'It won't be long now,' he put his hand gently on her arm 'and I'm sure, now I know who it is, that you've nothing to worry about as far as Susi's safety is concerned. In fact I think a couple of amateurs like that will be glad to return her safely and get away. All they want is the cash . . . '

She longed to believe him. She couldn't even contemplate the future without Susi — loneliness, emptiness — so often people asked her if she was lonely, meaning did she miss the company of adults, of socialising and the bright lights — sometimes perhaps, but as long as she had Susi, anything was bearable. Real loneliness, she knew now, was the awful void left by the absence of the one person you truly loved and needed — as she did her little girl.

When the time came she watched David drive off to the station. Why on earth they had wanted him to go by train no one could guess, probably it was an idea lifted from some television play they'd seen — the bag with the money lay beside him on the seat. She turned back to the house, the summer heat like a tangible weight as she went into the cool of the sitting room.

Once more Sarah and Jo-Anne were in the pool. Mrs. Finlay brought her a cup of coffee — but all she could think about was Susi, wondering where she was, close by perhaps, or miles away — if she'd had anything to eat . . . then, shuddering, if the men had touched her, harmed her . . . she counted the hours since she had been snatched. Unbelievably few in reality, yet seeming like a lifetime.

She tried to swallow the coffee, but it stuck in her throat. She got up once more and looked at the painting of David's wife. Wandered to the window and watched the swimmers. Sarah had invited a few friends in and they were lying or sitting round the pool, drinking, laughing, quarrelling as if no drama, which seemed to her beyond belief, was being enacted on their doorstep.

It hadn't been so difficult when David was there, finding things for her to do, talking, keeping her mind and hands occupied. How kind he was — beyond the demands of common humanity — as if he really cared, was really interested . . .

At last she heard his car returning . . . She ran out on the terrace to meet him. He took her hands in his, 'Well, we've done our part, carried it out to the letter, now all we have to do is wait a little while . . . '

For a moment a kind of anger flared inside her, 'That's all we've done for the past goodness knows how many hours . . . that's all anyone tells me . . . wait wait wait . . . ' Her voice rose on a note of hysteria. He drew her into the circle of his arm.

'I know — do believe me I understand, I can imagine exactly how you feel, but we are doing everything humanly possible. Unfortunately I couldn't wait to see who picked up the case, my instructions were to get straight on to the next local train and return to where I'd parked the car. But by now I expect they are counting the money — maybe not even waiting to do that before they get away — and they will want to deliver Susi safely just as soon as they can . . . '

She turned away, the tears flowing freely down her cheeks now. 'I wish I could believe you,' she said between sobs.

But the fact of his presence reassured her, he seemed so confident as he glanced at his watch. 'I have a feeling Susi will be back with you within the hour,' he grinned and for a moment she caught some of his confidence. 'I think you'll find that by now they're just a couple of scared lads — Sid wasn't very old and probably by now he regrets taking part in the thing at all. He was always a bit impulsive from what I remember, may even have been led on by the other one, whoever he is.'

He unlocked the safe. 'Might as well take the rest of the money back to the bank, no point in keeping it hanging around.' His back was towards her as he packed the notes back in their small case. She opened her mouth to beg him not to leave her just now, to wait at least until they heard something from the police, but she changed her mind, she already owed him so much, she must try now to rely on her own resources, meagre as they were . . .

He had hardly been gone half an

hour before once more she heard the sound of a car in the drive. Surely it couldn't be him so soon . . . she ran to the window. It was a police car. For a moment she closed her eyes — was this to be the moment of truth, the moment when they had come to tell her Susi was dead . . . or mutilated in some terrible way as she had imagined over and over again in her mind . . . violated perhaps, even her mind unbalanced by horror, terror and disgust at what they might have done . . . for a moment she thought she would faint. Then she heard the car door open and saw a policewoman get out, Huggy Bear in her arms . . . and then behind her Susi, dirty, dishevelled, but laughing up at the woman who held her hand, reaching out for Huggy Bear, and then turning round, and catching sight of Alison shrieking —

'Mummy! Look! Isn't it super? Just like on the telly — one of those 'HEE-HAW' cars with all the lights flashing. The sergeant let me press the switch — although they're not really meant to use them 'cept in a 'mergency. Just wait till I tell that Marcia at school, bet she never went in a police car with real fuzz!'

Alison crouched down on the gravel of the drive, her arms open wide, as the child dashed at her, and for a moment neither of them spoke while tears of joy and relief beyond measure ran down Alison's face and at last, pushing the hair back from her eyes, she knew such a feeling of peace it seemed she would almost die of it . . .

8

Just at that moment David arrived back and jumped out of the car when he caught sight of Susi — standing to watch mother and daughter as they greeted each other . . .

He could see from the strained expression on her face that Alison was near breaking point now and swiftly he stepped forward. 'Please may I be introduced?' Gravely he held out his hand toward Huggy Bear. Susi gave him a dazzling smile, reminding him sharply of her mother . . .

Alison got slowly to her feet, still grasping Susi's hand as if terrified to let her go. Her lashes clung together with the tears that she tried to brush away as she said 'Susi, this is David — Mr. Beresford. Somehow we've got to try and thank him for what he's done for us . . . ' then she turned to David, 'this is Susi, and of course, Huggy Bear,' she gave an attempt at a watery smile. Then she bent down again to the child.

'Are you all right sweetie? Your dress is all torn and your face dirty . . . they didn't . . . didn't hurt you did they?'

Over Susi's head the policewoman shook her head, 'No Mrs. Ross, apart from being a bit grubby, you've nothing to worry about . . . ' Alison realised the phrase held a world of meaning to reassure her that physically the child was unharmed.

Susi looked up at her, grinning widely. 'I had quite a super time Mum, we had baked beans for breakfast as well as supper and they let me stay up and watch the telly till the little white dot came on. I'd never seen it before. Colour it was too, can we paint our old black and white set do you think?'

David realised it was taking all Alison's strength to keep a grip on herself and not break down in front of the child, she needed a few minutes' respite to recover. He said, 'How about you and me going in to look at the telly now while Mummy gets us a cup of tea, eh?'

The policewoman said, 'Inspector Bond will be coming in later Mr. Beresford, whether there's any news or not of the capture of the kidnappers, he'll want to take a statement from Susi . . . '

David frowned. 'Is that really necessary,' then he shrugged, 'well of course I suppose it must be, and it doesn't look at the moment as though it's going to cause her much distress.'

The woman smiled. 'No, she seems to have been the only one who wasn't in the least worried. They left her outside the police station with some woman who was waiting for a bus. Apparently jumped out of a car and just pushed the child towards her, saying they were expecting her in the police station and would she take her in as they had to catch a plane and were running late!'

David gave a little gesture of impatience. 'I just don't understand the nerve of these villains, nothing seems to daunt them. Still, as far as this affair is concerned I suppose we could say all is well that ends well . . . '

The woman got back into the car and with a wave of her hand, was driven away. Alison still stood as though unaware of all that was going on around her, aware only of the fact that Susi was back safe and unharmed. She couldn't really accept it, feeling certain that in a moment she'd wake to find it a dream, just as she had thought at first the kidnapping had been an evil dream . . .

David gave her a gentle push towards the house. 'Could you be so very kind as to go and ask Mrs. Finlay to make us some tea do you think? And how about cucumber sandwiches and eclairs Susi? Do you think Huggy would approve of that kind of nosh?'

Susi looked up at him solemnly for a moment, then she said slowly, 'Yes please. He likes you,' she put her head on one side and considered him for a moment, then said, like a wise grown up, 'and he's never wrong. If Huggy likes you then I like you — and Mummy does too I expect . . . '

He laughed and took her hand. 'Come along then . . . '

As if Susi's words had suddenly brought her to life, Alison said quickly, 'I really ought to clean her up a bit first, find some fresh clothes before she has any tea . . . '

'I'll take her into the downstairs cloakroom to wash her hands and face, that'll do for now, once she's had some tea we'll see about some clothes of Jo-Anne's and a bath . . . ' Now he spoke with his usual authority, this he could do, organise, decide, direct — in the nicest possible way, for he could see Alison was going to have to be helped over the next few hours, almost as much as she had been over the past days and nights. She was still like a ship without a rudder, almost as shocked by the fact of Susi's swift return, unharmed, as she had been by her disappearance. Quite obviously her

136

imagination had had Susi dead, or at the best, maimed in some way, and deeply frightened, but in fact nothing bad had happened to her, to her it had just been a game, a great adventure, she'd enjoyed the whole thing and it had even been gift wrapped as you might say, by the ride in the police car. But he knew that Alison still could hardly accept this, she was still half looking for something sinister.

Alison went into the house and crossed the hall to the kitchen quarters. Mrs. Finlay was rolling out pastry for the evening meal and looked up in surprise when she saw Alison. It was seldom any of the family came into the kitchen, much to her disappointment as there was nothing she liked better than a good gossip.

'Is there any news of the little girl, Mrs. Ross?' She pushed the hair back from her forehead with one hand, leaving a streak of flour down one cheek. For a brief moment Alison looked at her without speaking, her reflexes were still slow. Then she smiled, 'Of course you haven't heard. They brought her back, just this moment . . . she's all right, they haven't . . . didn't do her any harm at all. Isn't it wonderful?'

She sank down in the nearest chair as if her legs would no longer support her and now the tears rolled down her cheeks — tears of relief . . .

'There there,' Mrs. Finlay fussed round like a hen that had hatched out a duckling. She handed Alison a tissue and then turned to the stove and put on the kettle. 'A nice cup of tea, that's what you need. Where's the bairn now?'

Alison smiled tremulously. 'With Mr. Beresford, that's why I've come. He sent me to ask you for tea for the three of us, and cucumber sandwiches and eclairs . . . ' she repeated the message rather like a well versed child. Then added, 'I don't really think the food's necessary, Susi seems to have been quite well fed, even if it was an undiluted diet of beans on toast — and

I can see you're busy . . . '

'That's true, but if I show you where the things are, you could cut the sandwiches for me, Miss, while I get out the cakes and make the tea . . . ' She too realised Alison needed something to occupy her hands and take her mind off the events of the last few hours.

Gratefully the girl got to her feet and started to slice the brown bread Mrs. Finlay put on the table, spreading it deftly and neatly, her quickness not going unobserved by the older woman. She cut thin slivers of cucumber, soaked them for a moment in vinegar, and lightly peppered them, all of which met with Mrs. Finlay's nodding approval. This girl was different as chalk from cheese from Miss Sarah. She gave an involuntary sniff — that little madam wanted her bottom smacked in her opinion. Still, she couldn't altogether blame the girl, her Dad had made her into a real spoilt mess — and the kiddie, Jo-Anne would soon be in the same mould if there either wasn't another baby to put her nose out of joint, or someone took her in hand . . . she guessed this one's child was well behaved and properly disciplined. You could soon tell. Judge a parent by the child's behaviour she always said. Most delinquency these days she reckoned you could pin on the home life . . .

She laid up the trolley, arranged the eclairs on a lace doily, and said, 'Shall I wheel it in Miss, or will you?'

Alison washed her hands at the sink, ran her fingers through her hair, she felt a thorough mess, like Susi looked. After tea perhaps she'd have the energy to tidy up a bit, both of them. 'I'll take it, and thank you so much . . . '

The woman held open the swing door as she pushed the trolley across the hall. It was noiseless on its rubber wheels so that the two in the sitting room didn't hear her. They sat side by side on the deep sofa, Susi leaning against David. Huggy Bear clasped tightly to her, watching Dougal as he went round and round with Brian on the Roundabout. Susi was gurgling with delight and looking up at David now and then to make sure he was enjoying it too. Alison felt the stupid tears once more behind her lids . . . they looked so right together, it just didn't seem possible . . .

'Tea's up you two,' she said rattling the cups. Dougal faded into the distance and David turned off the set.

Susi ran to her mother. 'Mummy have you ever seen such a big set? Isn't it super? Can I stay up late and see some more please? I'm not a bit tired.' Alison smoothed the child's hair back from her flushed face, it was tangled and matted, she supposed it hadn't been combed since they had picked her up . . . 'No darling, it's early bed for you and we have to get you cleaned up. And Huggy. Whatever kind of place was it they took you to?'

Susi had settled back comfortably on the sofa, completely relaxed with the confidence of childhood. For a moment Alison envied her. Solemnly David handed her the plate of sandwiches, suggesting she take two, one for Huggy. Looking up at him with her wide smile she said, 'You're quite the nicest man I ever met, isn't he Mum?'

Alison bent over the tea pot pretending not to hear.

'Shall I put sugar in yours David?'

He nodded, 'Just one please, and lemon, not milk.'

'I didn't know people put real lemon in tea ever,' Susi said, bright eyed with curiosity.

Alison frowned at her, 'It's very rude to make personal remarks about what people eat or drink, darling.'

'Sorry Mummy. It was Huggy wanted to know really,' she giggled and bit into the crisp cucumber with relish.

David leant back with a feeling of deep content as he watched the child tucking into the cakes and sandwiches. She ate neatly and cleanly as he had imagined a child of Alison's would, drinking her milk and offering the mug to Huggy, who also had a piece of cake and some sandwiches on a plate in front of him. Her correction of the child, a gentle chiding, had not gone unnoticed — had it been Sarah and Jo-Anne under the circumstances, she would have been fussing round and over indulging her . . .

He felt a stab of annoyance hearing a car arrive and the Inspector and Sergeant were brought into the room by Mrs. Finlay. He got up slowly, reluctantly, impatient at having the cosy scene destroyed by their intrusion . . .

'Might I just have a word,' the Inspector said, raising his eyebrows at Susi . . . and adding, 'on your own please Mr. Beresford.'

'We'll go into the library,' David said shortly. He turned to Alison and Susi, 'please excuse me ladies — and gentleman,' he bowed gravely in Huggy's direction, 'I shan't be a moment, then we'll see about that bath and some fresh clothes.' He looked across at Mrs.

Finlay. 'Perhaps you'd have a look in Miss Sarah's closet, she and Brian have gone sailing this afternoon, and won't be back till late. Let Mrs. Ross have something for herself and Susi please.'

In the library the Inspector said, 'I've got some excellent news sir. It seems that directly the kidnappers had dropped the child at the bus stop, they couldn't wait to spend some of the cash, went into the off licence just by the police station, bought a carton of beer cans, whisky and cigarettes, and gave the man a twenty pound note from the ransom money. We'd already circulated the numbers as you know, his assistant slipped out at the back to phone on the pretext of finding a big enough carton for the bottles and so on, and we picked them up just like that. They're down at the station now, it's much as I thought, and as you suggested sir, a couple of layabouts, amateurs, the one the lorry driver you dismissed, and the other a scrap dealer we've had suspicions about for some time. Shacked up with a couple of tarts in an old deserted farmhouse not far from here — that's where they took the child . . . '

'No wonder she's pretty grubby,' David smiled.

The Inspector nodded, but he didn't smile. 'We were lucky sir in this case, dead lucky. If they'd been a bit more professional and less frightened when they found they'd made a hash of it, I wouldn't like to have gambled on the safety of the child — not that I would have said anything of course — but these cases can be very tricky, like sitting on dynamite . . . '

David nodded. 'So that's all there is to it. It's fallen flat on its face as you might say, and I'll even get my money back, eh?'

'Yes sir, in time, these things take time. There'll be certain formalities to observe of course, they have to be charged, and we'll need to take a statement from the child . . . but I don't imagine that'll involve much grief.'

'Will it really be necessary?' David was thinking of Alison as much as Susi, although the child might well be made to think things she need not have known about . . .

The Inspector looked at him quickly, 'Maybe I'll let Sergeant Mitchell do that part, he has a child of his own,' for just a moment a brief smile flitted across his usually sombre features.

'That might be an idea, whatever happens we don't want to frighten her, to let her think she was in any danger even, as the thought doesn't seem to have occurred to her.'

'No, sir, in any case it will be later on, once she has returned home with her mother, and we have statements from the two villains. There is no immediacy.'

'Certainly not,' David said, more sharply than he intended.

For a moment he had forgotten Alison would be leaving, taking Susi and Huggy Bear with her.

Being reminded of it was not pleasant — not at all pleasant . . .

9

Alison sat watching Susi as she ate her tea, still scarcely able to believe she was back, safe and unharmed. As if she were conscious of her mother's gaze, the child looked up, clambered off the sofa, and went over to put her arms round her neck.

'I missed you Mummy — but wasn't it a bit of luck I had Huggy for company? They were such funny men, one of them was quite nice, I didn't like the other though, he smelt. The one who drove the lorry said he'd once had a little girl just like me, but she'd gone away with her Mummy — and do you know he cried? I'd never seen a man cry before. I thought they never did . . . that it was only girls.'

Alison buried her face in the child's soft neck and thought, 'Thank God he did have a child, maybe that's why he made sure you came back safely to me, my darling . . . '

She got to her feet. 'Now you must get cleaned up, love.' She felt uncertain now, not sure what her position was in regard to David . . . now the emergency was over. She knew he would be getting his money back, and the great cloud of tragedy and drama had been lifted from her. Now she felt she must get home, pick up the threads of life as it would have to be lived again, return to normal as quickly as possible.

David came back into the room from seeing the two policemen off. 'That's O.K. then, all weighed and paid as they say in Devon. They'll bring the money back within a day or two. They'll want to ask Susi one or two questions, but nothing very alarming . . . now where were you three off to, eh?'

Alison looked at him gravely, 'We must go home. I see they've brought back my car, and I already owe you so much, I don't know how to thank you, how to repay you . . . '

'Then don't try,' he said quietly, 'the best way you can show your appreciation, if that's what you wish, is to stay at least for tonight so I can enjoy the delightful company of Susi — and of course Huggy Bear.' He took both her hands in his, 'I want you to have a good night's sleep, my dear, something you haven't had the last couple of nights I'm sure — I want you all to be comfortable and safe and well looked after . . . that isn't much to ask is it?' He grinned like a small boy.

Alison smiled 'Of course not . . . '

'Then come on, let's find Mrs. Finlay and some clean clothes, and the bathroom, I'm sure Huggy wants to wash his paws, he's obviously a fastidious bear . . . '

Susi skipped joyously along behind him. 'What's that word you said . . . fastiddy something, mean?'

'Fastidious . . . very particular,' he said, ruffling her hair.

She nodded, 'Oh yes, he's that all right, just like Mummy . . . '

Alison had to admit it was with a sense of relief she accepted the suggestion. She felt drained of all energy and emotion, as if her brain was only working at half its usual speed, and the thought of organising food, and hot water and clean clothes seemed at the moment an overwhelming task she just could not face.

David joined them on the landing after he'd been to see Mrs. Finlay about the clothes. Susi rushed from gadget to gadget in the blue bathroom leading off the bedroom Alison had slept in, giving little cries of delight, explaining to Huggy what they were and how they worked.

'Can we have a shower, Mummy?'

Alison shook her head, 'No my love, you're going into a nice deep hot bath to be thoroughly scrubbed.'

'Then can I have some of that blue oil stuff in the water?'

David said, 'Of course, and here's Glenda Goose, I haven't seen Jo-Anne use her for months so I'm sure she

150

won't miss her. If you put her in the water she floats and you can lay the soap on that flat space on her back see?'

He turned away, not sure if he might embarrass them with his presence, he realised neither of them were used to male company at home, probably Susi had never had anyone but her mother present when she was bathed — and even small girls had their modesty. But to his delight Susi caught hold of his hand.

'Please stay and show me how Glenda Goose floats, and where to put the soap.' She looked up at him with her mother's eyes . . .

'I'd love to, that is if Mummy doesn't think I'll be in the way.' Alison laughed, 'You may get splashed, bath time can be quite a ball.'

He sat on the stool by the bath while Alison scrubbed Susi, soaping her hair and making the child giggle with delight as she tickled her toes. David threw back his head and roared with laughter, the child's wonderful, carefree joy was infectious.

Suddenly, as Alison watched him, she realised how much she missed having a man — a father for Susi, a husband for herself — the warmth and intimacy, the hundreds of little things that built up into a marriage between two people . . . specially when they had a child — and she hadn't seen Susi so happy, so completely joyous and at ease, usually she was inclined to be a little shy, to clam up with any men she encountered. It was natural she supposed, she was a mother's child from necessity, not choice . . . but now she was opening and unfurling like a blossom in the sunshine, and Alison felt a stab of grief that it would all have to end so soon.

At last she said it was time Susi came out of the warm blue water. Reluctantly the child stood up and Alison wrapped her in the enormous bath sheet.

'Let me dry her,' David said 'while you collect the clothes, I left them on the bed with Huggy in charge.'

Alison went through into the bedroom, listening to the squeals of delight as David rubbed Susi's back with a 'rub a dub dub, three men in a tub,' routine, which she hadn't heard herself since she was a small girl ... the lump returned to her throat as she picked up the quilted dressing gown in palest blue with slippers to match, the delicate silk nightie embroidered with flowers and fairies, pressing its softness against her face for a moment. Then she went back into the bathroom and held them up for Susi to see.

'Oh Mummy, they're quite the loveliest things I ever saw ... it's just like having a birthday. Do they belong to your little girl, Uncle David?'

He shook his head smiling, 'My little girl's little girl — my granddaughter.'

She turned to Alison 'Have I got a grandfather, Mummy?'

For a moment Alison looked away as she felt the warm tears behind her lids — then she said, 'No darling, I'm afraid not.'

'Then I'll have to make do with you,' the child said to David, with charming candour, and he nodded, smiling too. Alison tried not to think of how she was going to explain to Susi that there would soon be a time when Uncle David, substitute grandfather or not, would not be with them.

She felt his eyes on her, and noticed a great compassion in them, and perhaps something more — pity maybe . . . if so she didn't want pity, she had managed without it — it could destroy your self confidence, the barrier she had built round the two of them. She could not know that David too was having his own private thoughts of how it felt to be part and parcel of such a warm, involving relationship. He loved Alison's attitude to her child, and Susi's to her mother. Somehow they both seemed to emanate a completely happy feeling that he had never achieved with his own daughter and Jo-Anne, much as he loved them. That, though, could be his own fault for giving them too much, too easily. They hadn't had to evaluate life and human relationships to find that nothing came easy that was worth having, as this perfect relationship that existed between mother and child, and now even more than before he realised what terrible mental anguish Alison must have suffered when Susi was snatched from her — almost a physical hurt.

Now he picked up the child and put her in the big double bed.

'Even blue sheets and blankets, Mummy. Isn't it heavenly? Like sleeping in a flower bed of forget-me-nots . . . '

Alison nodded, pouring the warm milk from the thermos Mrs. Finlay had brought, with a plate of milk chocolate digestive biscuits . . . 'and my very favourite biscuits — next to orange milk chocolate of course, but really Huggy likes those better than I do — he's very fastiddy-what-you-said, Uncle David, me, I'm easier to please.'

David regarded her gravely, 'Of course.'

She snuggled down under the clothes and already her eyelids were starting to droop, but she made a valiant effort as she said, 'Please, unless Mummy is going to read to me, would you tell me a story, Uncle David?'

He cleared his throat, taking his glasses out of his breast pocket and swinging them round and round as he concentrated . . . Alison could imagine it was just the way he looked at a board meeting, or a gathering of shareholders . . .

'This is the story of H.R . . . ' he began . . .

'H.R . . . who's that?' Susi became alert once more, her interest aroused.

'H.R. is Helpful Rabbit — you must often have seen the letters up beside the road along the motorways and main roads down here in Devon . . . '

Susi nodded, 'Yes I have, I asked Mummy what they meant and she said it stood for Holiday Route for the people coming from other parts of England so they'd know where to go to avoid the traffic . . . '

'And Mummy was quite right, but it does also stand for Helpful Rabbit, who often has to direct lost travellers, and of course he was very proud when he found his initials had been put up in so many public places . . . '

Susi sipped her milk with a look of absorbed interest on her face. 'He had several very good friends who lived on a farm quite near, down a muddy lane, across some fields and into the woods, where bluebells and primroses grow in spring — there was Glenda Goose and her husband, who spent much of their time in the pond in the middle of the farmyard, then there was James Alexander Aloysius Crow . . . ' he stopped for a moment as Susi gave a yelp of delighted laughter . . . 'What a name for a crow!'

'Oh all his family had distinguished names, it was only his distant cousins who lived in the high rise flats in the elms on the edge of the main road who had ordinary names like Tom, Dick and Harry . . . '

Alison sat on the end of the bed, the evening sun slanting through the french windows, open to the balcony, catching the lights in Susi's newly washed hair, and on the dark head so close to hers, his glasses in his hand still as he made up the story as he went along, an outrageously funny story which, now she had finished her milk, made Susi roll about the bed with laughter. For a moment she was tempted to protest that the child would never sleep, but she couldn't spoil their pleasure, and it had to be admitted — her own — for she gazed at him wide eyed, it seemed impossible that this delightfully relaxed and humorous man could also be the boss, the big man who kept making money, the all powerful man whose name was a byword in the area — he just didn't seem the same person as the one of whom she had caught the odd glimpse at the office, a man who indeed walked the corridors of power.

At last the story came to a satisfactory conclusion, and David put Susi gently from him, for by now she had snuggled into the curve of his arm, her head on his shoulder as she listened. He sat back on his heels beside the low bed, and said smiling, 'Now, if you are lying comfortably Susi, it's time you went to sleep . . . '

'Will there be more of the story please, Uncle David?'

He grinned 'I think there'll have to be, we can't leave poor H.R. suspended in time can we?' He thought how delightful it was to find a child who preferred a story, however simple, to the everlasting television, as Jo-Anne did, shrugging off any attempt he had made in the past to tell her a story . . .

Now Susi gave a little contented nod and slid down into the softness of the big bed, and almost immediately her eyes closed, the curved lashes dark on her cheek. Alison and David stood side by side watching her, and for the first time that she could recall, Alison saw that Huggy Bear lay forgotten on the floor, not clasped in Susi's arms . . .

Was it because David had, for a few brief moments, fulfilled the empty role of a non existent father?

She wasn't sure if the thought brought her pain or pleasure . . .

10

Alison had felt certain she wouldn't be able to sleep after a day of such tension, excitement and eventual joy, but, like Susi, almost as soon as her head touched the pillow, she drifted away, one arm round the little girl, who had now reinstated Huggy Bear to his rightful position in the crook of her arm.

After what seemed only a few moments she was woken by Susi tickling her nose with one of Huggy's paws. 'Mummy, it's after eight, and I can hear someone out in the garden. Can I get dressed and go and play?'

Alison struggled up through the mists of sleep and glanced at her watch. As she did so there was a discreet knock on the door and Mrs. Finlay came in with a breakfast tray, loaded with food — fresh grapefruit, eggs and bacon on a chafing dish, toast, marmalade, and a pot of coffee.

She put it down on a low table by the french windows and drew up two chairs. 'Mr. Beresford's orders, Miss, you and the young lady to have your breakfast quietly here, he'll be up later to see you.' She glanced at Susi who stood with Huggy Bear clasped to her, 'and I hope you slept well, Miss Susi, and no worse for your adventure,' she smiled.

Susi gave her a wide smile in return, and said, 'No, we're fine, in fact Huggy and I quite enjoyed ourselves,' she turned to Alison and took her hand, 'if it hadn't been that we knew Mummy would be worrying . . . and I had to ride in a police car with the lights and the hee haw going . . .'

The woman glanced at Alison, shaking her head, 'Kids today, they don't seem to . . . well, they just take everything in their stride . . . ' She went towards the door, 'enjoy your breakfast, I expect that bear's hungry too, I put a small plate and cup on the tray for him . . . '

Susi ran to the table and saw the tiny china with flowers painted on it, obviously some of Jo Anne's toys. 'Ooh how super, thank you. Huggy likes you, Mrs Finlay . . . '

Alison started to protest, picking up the clothes and shoes from where they were scattered round the room, 'But I must get to the office, and take Susi to Playschool, I've had quite enough time off as it is . . . '

Mrs Finlay said 'I don't know about that I'm sure Miss, after what you've been through I should think you need some rest and quiet, but I should leave it to Mr Beresford, he knows best . . . '

Alison sipped the coffee, ate the grapefruit, but couldn't face the egg and bacon, however Susi with the healthy appetite of childhood, managed both portions with no difficulty, almost forgetting that Huggy had to be fed too.

They had just finished dressing when David knocked on the door and entered

163

to Alison's call of 'Please come in.'

'Well,' he smiled 'that's better, a very lively looking trio this morning, I hope you all slept well.'

Susi ran to him and spontaneously put her arms round him. He lifted her up and kissed her.

'Uncle David, will there be some more about H.R. tonight please?'

He glanced at Alison over her head, 'Well, I don't know about tonight . . . '

'Susi, don't be tiresome,' she said quickly, 'we have to go home, in fact we should really have gone last night . . . '

'I've arranged for you to have the day off,' he said quietly, 'give you time to go home and get yourselves straightened out a bit,' his eyes twinkled, 'If I know anything about it you'll start cleaning the flat from top to bottom, do an enormous wash, and visit the supermarket . . . '

Alison smiled. 'The first part might be right, but I still have all the stuff from the supermarket I bought before

. . . on Friday — in the boot of the car, I hope . . .'

She went over to the window and looked down the drive to where the little red Mini stood parked as the police had left it.

He nodded, 'Of course. Well I must be getting along myself,' he added briskly, returning to his other role of business executive at her words. 'I shall see you at the office tomorrow perhaps — and Susi, to you — au revoir . . . till we meet again — you, Huggy and I, and I hope, further instalments of H.R.'

He bent and kissed the child and for a moment her bottom lip quivered as if tears were not far away. Alison was surprised, she was a child who seldom cried, she realised how attached she must have become to David in the few hours she had known him. Children and animals had an instinctive reaction to loving kindness — and David was brimming over with it . . . she turned away and started to put their few belongings into the case, feeling her own tears not far away. She folded Jo-Anne's and Sara's clothes in a neat pile and left them on the end of the bed.

Her head still bent she said softly, 'I just can't begin to thank you for all you've done for Susi and me . . . I'm only glad you're getting the money back, at least that's some kind of compensation,' she swallowed, 'it's such an inadequate phrase, just thank you — but I mean so much more than that . . . '

He came over and took her hands now, pulling her round to face him, his eyes full of compassion. 'Look, my dear child, it is I who should be thanking you, not only for taking the rap which was meant for me and Sara, but also for your company,' he turned and looked at Susi 'and for introducing me to this charming pair of hostages . . . '

Reluctantly he dropped her hands, 'Well, I must go and get the wheels of industry turning again I suppose,' he made his tone light, hoping she

wouldn't notice the break in his voice
. . . in a way he regretted the weekend
was over . . . if only the actual
circumstances had been happier . . .

As Alison and Susi made their way
up the steep, narrow staircase to the
little flat under the roof, she felt as if
she'd been away for months, years
almost, as if she'd lived a whole life
time since she and Sara had picked up
her things . . .

She opened the front door and
glanced round. After the luxury and
spaciousness of Woodrising it seemed
like a cupboard, already stifling in the
summer morning heat . . . but it was
still home and their intimate belongings
were scattered around . . .

She busied herself tidying up, washing Susi's clothes, and her own
crumpled dress, making them some
lunch, promising to take her and Huggy
in the park later to feed the ducks and
go on the swings . . . all the time she
thought of the pool at Woodrising, of
the comfort, and she couldn't get the

memory of David's face, his voice, the touch of his hands, out of her mind . . . the tenderness and compassion he had shown, the way he was with Susi . . . she kept wondering what he was doing at this moment . . . 'It's quite ridiculous,' she told herself, 'but it's almost as though I am falling in love with him . . . and yet he has a daughter my own age, a grand daughter Susi's age . . . ' she gave an impatient shrug, 'pull yourself together Alison, it's because someone has been kind and thoughtful.'

But in spite of that, she felt panic — there couldn't be any future in it, they were world's apart. For the first time for months she thought of her brief affair with Susi's father . . . Johnnie had been in charge of the building of the new motorway, they'd met at a party, and she had fallen wildly, deeply, thrillingly in love, and believed everything he had promised about marriage and a life together — until she found she was pregnant,

168

and his wife had arrived on the scene . . .

At the time she had wanted only to die and vowed that never never would she believe what any other man told her, never let her heart rule her head — now she thought if she did ever love again, it could be David, or someone like him, someone kind and compassionate upon whom she could lean . . . she felt so weary, so unutterably weary — the kidnapping seemed to have sapped any energy she had entirely. But somehow she had to pick up the threads of life again, go back to the office and face the inevitable questions, the curiosity — all of it probably well meant, but somehow an intrusion of her privacy . . . of something which had become ineffably precious . . .

She dropped Susi at Playschool with strict instructions to wait indoors till she picked her up . . . She knew she was going to have to try to adjust, to suppress her anxiety about the child, but somehow she seemed to have become doubly precious now.

Joe Crump, the man from security who had helped her look for Susi, was the first to greet her, grasping her hand and shaking it.

'So glad about your little girl, Mrs. Ross, quite unharmed I hear . . . '

She nodded, 'Yes, you're very kind, and I must thank you for helping me, I'm afraid at the time I must have seemed very ungrateful.'

He grinned. 'One would hardly expect much else at a time like that, I got a grandchild about your Susi's age so I know how you must have felt . . . '

She ran on up to the General office. The girls were waiting, hardly able to keep their curiosity within the bounds of common courtesty as they all gazed at her . . .

'How are you?'

'How's Susi?'

'What happened?'

'How much ransom did old Beresford have to fork out? It didn't say in the paper . . . '

'There's a picture on the front page of the local of you, and one of Susi with her teddy bear, sweet it is . . . '

She went to her desk and took the cover off her typewriter, feeling the warm blood suffuse her neck and face. She didn't quite know why, it was foolish really, they meant well and it was a natural interest which she would surely have shown under similar circumstances, it was just that somehow, suddenly she felt like a hermit crab without its shell — vulnerable, as if they were able to see down inside her innermost soul, to read her thoughts, her feelings about David. It all felt so intensely personal, intensely private, making her feel unreasonably resentful of their probing . . .

She looked up at last, forcing a smile, 'Well really it all happened so quickly in a way, I can only say I felt numb, I hardly knew what I was doing but

171

everyone was so kind, the police, and Dav . . . Mr. Beresford . . . '

Did she detect an added interest in their eyes as she stumbled over his name, or was it her imagination sharpened by emotion . . .

'And is little Susan all right?' Miss Atwood, the head of the department, never used shortened names.

Alison nodded, glad of a slight change of subject.

'Oh yes she's fine. I think she really came off best of all, the whole thing was just a kind of game to her, specially the ride in the police car!'

'How very fortunate she was not aware of the danger she was in,' Miss Atwood said primly, then she turned to the others, 'come along girls, back to work, all the excitement is over now, business as usual please . . . '

As she spoke the door from the corridor opened and David came in.

It was as if a film had stopped suddenly, freezing all the characters into immobility. No one moved or spoke as he stood in the doorway, his eyes gazing round the room, from one girl to another, until they came to rest on Alison. None of them could remember the great Mr. Beresford coming into the General Office ever before. He had his own personal assistant, his own staff, and they lived behind frosted glass in the inner sanctum.

Miss Atwood, like an anxious sheep dog, shepherded her flock to its place and stepped forward to take the file which David held in his hand.

'Good morning sir. Can I be of some assistance?' She bridled as he looked at her, then he smiled.

'Thank you so much, but no, I just wanted to ask Mrs. Ross to do a small job for me. I'm sure you will have no objection . . . '

Miss Atwood's expression changed, a frown knitting her brows, she had never known the boss address himself to one of her typists, and certainly protocol directed it should only be through her if he did . . . before she could protest

David had brushed past her and stood in front of Alison, laying the file on her desk.

'Good morning, Mrs. Ross,' his eyes held hers for a moment, but she was unable to read the expression in them for the confusion that filled her, the conflicting emotions that chased through her mind, her heart had given a lurch when she saw him, dressed in his business suit, immaculate, the perfect tycoon. In complete contrast to the David who had sat on Susi's bed in slacks and shirt, swinging his glasses in one hand while he told her a story.

She felt a flood of affection tinged with embarrassment as she realised all the other girls were staring from their places, unable even now to absorb the fact that he had come to talk to one of their members . . .

David went on talking, but Alison was hardly conscious of the words. It must have been as obvious to everyone as well as to her that the file was simply a pretext to come and see her . . . 'so I thought perhaps you would look up the files for me,' she heard him say in conclusion as he laid the folder down.

Before she could reply he had turned and left as swiftly as he had arrived. She knew all the girls were staring at her as she bent her head over the file and opened it.

There were several typewritten sheets, and a request to look up some details from the personnel office about the lorry driver . . . but pinned to the top was one torn from a diary, and in his own handwriting he had written . . . 'Please have dinner with me tonight — if there is any difficulty over a baby sitter for Susi, you can bring her here for the night. D.B.'

She sat staring at the note until she felt rather than saw Miss Atwood standing by her desk, her hand held out. Quickly she tore the note from the clip and turned it over.

'May I see what Mr. Beresford requires, Mrs. Ross?'

Alison passed her the file with the

175

request for information. She read it and sniffed, 'I should have thought his own staff could deal with this without bothering my girls,' she said, 'however if that is what he wants, then you'd better do it before getting on with your other work. But hurry up, we are already behind as a result of various delays and hold ups.'

She turned away sharply and Alison knew it was a veiled reprimand to her for causing an upset in the usual smooth running of the office, on which the woman prided herself. For a moment she felt sorry for her, poor woman, she had nothing else to interest her . . .

But she didn't care at the moment about anyone or anything else — David had asked her out and a little jet of pure happiness started up inside her. At once her mind flew to her scanty wardrobe as she wondered what kind of restaurant he would take her to, whether she should wear the long black skirt and the lace blouse she had made from a cheap remnant, or the short silk dress which had a tear in the skirt, mended, but still obvious . . . and she would have to ring round in the lunch hour to find someone to sit with Susi, she felt she couldn't ask David for more favours by dumping Susi on his household once more . . . But most of all she felt a lightness of heart, an elation at the thought of seeing him again as David, not as Mr. Beresford of Beresford Enterprises . . .

She picked up the folder and went out of the General office and along the corridor to where the files were kept. As she worked she realised the information he had asked for was really irrelevant — just an excuse for his contact with her — she had to smile, it was rather like a teenage tryst — a boy meets girl affair, the kind that started by his asking to carry her books home from school, but whatever it might resemble, it made her feel somehow cherished and younger than she had for years . . .

Putting the papers back in the folder

she went along to his suite of offices and knocked on the outer door, remembering sharply the last time she had been there and the cause of it . . . She had kept his note in her pocket in case the girl should open the folder before she passed it to him, hoping she would be allowed to deliver it herself. She had only seen Miss Passmore, his secretary, once, but she seemed a very different kettle of fish from Miss Atwood, and now she smiled at Alison and said, 'Mr. Beresford is expecting you, will you go in?' and added, 'I'm so glad your little girl is safe and well, it must have been a terrible time for you.'

Alison smiled and thanked her, and went into the inner office.

It was softly carpeted with an enormous desk, a trough of green plants, and several original water colours on the wall — she guessed it was his taste, not that of some disinterested commercial decorator — it had the same feel as Woodrising.

He was standing looking out of the

window, across the quarry and up to where the tors and hills of Dartmoor shimmered in the summer heat. He swung round as he heard the door close softly.

'Hullo. I was just looking longingly at the moor, I'm a complete addict, and as I did so a phrase ran through my head — it's odd, do you sometimes think of some words, or a quotation, and feel unsure whether they are original or if you read them?'

She nodded. 'Yes, but usually with me it's someone else's words, not mine . . . '

He grinned. 'Probably these are — but they're rather lovely — see if you know them . . . Come with me and I will show you morning on a thousand hills . . . '

She shook her head slowly. 'They're beautiful, but unfamiliar . . . '

'I was thinking of Hameldown and how the larks would be singing,' he paused, holding out his hand for the file, 'anyway I hope I didn't set you too onerous a task,' his eyes twinkled.

She grinned. 'Well it was rather hard work . . . but thank you for the lovely invitation, I've love to come, and I can easily solve the baby sitting problem, thanks all the same for your suggestion . . . '

'Fine,' his face lit up, 'tell you what, I'll call for you fairly early if I may, and perhaps Susi and I could have a little session with H.R. I feel that rabbit is going places and must be dug up out of the limbo he sank into last time. Will that be O.K.?'

'Lovely. What time can I expect you?'

'About seven. I'll order dinner for half past eight so that gives us plenty of time, and don't worry about dressing up, I'm going to take you to a delightful little pub on the edge of the moor, kept by a friend of mine where relaxation, good food and drink, and a homely atmosphere are the keynotes . . . '

As he spoke now the phone on his desk rang and she went out of the office feeling as though she were indeed riding on cloud nine . . . once again aware of the sweet sensitivity he possessed for she guessed his remarks about not dressing up had arisen from the sure knowledge that her wardrobe was very limited . . .

She went back to her typing with a light step, only partly dimmed by the frigid attitude of Miss Atwood, and the curious stares of the other girls . . .

But at long last the afternoon drew to a close, it was time to go and fetch Susi and to get ready for her date. She covered her typewriter and went along the corridor to the cloakroom . . .

It was as she stood in the little cubicle washing her hands, hidden from the rest of the cloakroom that she heard two girls come in and start to talk and laugh — and suddenly her own name dropped like a stone into a pool, the ripples of chatter ever widening . . .

11

She stood frozen into immobility as she heard the voices, and the words gradually sunk in.

They were two juniors, one from her own department and the other from Accounts. She recognised their voices ... the first one was called Pam ...

'Quite a bit of excitement for once in this dull backwater eh Rosie? Kidnapping. Only wants a nice juicy murder and we'll all be on the telly.'

'You are the limit — you never know, it might be you gets murdered!'

'Not likely, my Dad says it's only certain types of girls that get themselves killed ... '

'What sort then?'

'You know, the easy kind, prostitutes ... '

'You are awful, there aren't any of that sort in Ashleigh any road ... ' The one called Rosie lowered her voice then although Alison knew she was unaware anyone else was in the room. She stood, her hands still wet, not daring to move as her own name was mentioned.

'Still, I must say Alison hasn't done badly for herself now the kid's back I mean. It's pretty obvious old Beresford's interest,' she giggled, 'wonder what went on back at the big house — after all she was there a couple of nights, and you know what men his age are like . . . '

Pam said quickly, 'I think that's a rotten thing to say, I feel sorry for Ali with a kid and all to bring up . . . '

'Still you know what they say, another slice off a cut loaf's never missed,' Rose gave another giggle.

'I've never heard it and I don't know what it means anyway.'

'Well, everyone knows she never married, the kid's illegitimate and if she'll do it once she'll do it again, specially when you think what's in it for her.'

'Look who's talking! Anyone 'ud think you were pure as the driven snow, Blessed are they who are never found out I say . . . '

'That's different, Mark and I are engaged and everyone has sex before marriage these days. Don't you know it's the permissive age?'

'I don't think Ali's like that, she never goes out anywhere and Susi's a nice kid, she's brought her up jolly well, can't be much fun on your own.'

'Yes, well I'm only saying she's still lucky to have hooked D.B. I know it wasn't exactly lucky to have Susi kidnapped — I'm not saying that — but she's bound to be making the most of it, stands to reason, and old Atwood was properly thrown when he came into the office, I don't ever remember seeing him in there before. It was obvious he'd only come to see Ali. Wouldn't mind betting he's dating her now too . . . after all she's only a clerk like you and me, just a bit older that's all . . . '

Alison put out her hand to steady

herself against the basin, praying the girls wouldn't come into the cubicle, looking round wildly for some means of escape — desperate like a hunted animal, unable to think what she would do or say if they confronted her . . .

With relief she heard the clasps of their handbags snap to and the sound of the door opening and closing as they hurried out into the corridor. She waited till their footsteps had receded down the stairs, her face burning as she recalled their words . . . 'She's lucky to have hooked D.B . . . '

She stumbled down the stairs and out into the summer evening, slumping down in the driving seat of the Mini and sitting for a moment, trying to pull herself together . . . it was as if someone had hit her on the head, she felt thunderstruck. Nothing had been further from her mind than the thought of 'catching' David, of hooking him as the girl had said. Of course she found him attractive, that was undeniable, it had been marvellous to have someone to lean on and when he had been with Susi, talking to her, telling her a story, naturally it had crossed her mind how wonderful it would be for Susi to have a father — even if he were a stepfather — but in a way it had been an impersonal thought — it just happened that David was there at the moment — reliable, a very present help in trouble, tender and sensitive with the child — and what woman didn't long for security if she were honest — specially with a small girl to bring up. But as for actually thinking of David in terms of hard cash, as a meal ticket and more, the idea hadn't even entered her head till now, it had been a purely emotional thing, born perhaps from gratitude as much as anything. Now she felt a raw open wound that the girls' remarks had made, she cringed from the idea that people were talking this way, saying and believing that she had made a play for the boss deliberately. How could they? It was as if they thought she had deliberately arranged for Susi to be kidnapped in place of Jo-Anne. She felt besmirched . . . all the joy had drained away . . .

Despair swept over her at the thought of the atmosphere in the office, the feeling all the time that people would be gossiping and giggling behind her back. She dropped her head on her hands on the steering wheel, unutterably weary, it was as if the poison from their words was seeping right through her . . . she heard people now starting to leave the offices. She started the engine, she must hurry or she'd be late for Susi . . .

As she drove her thoughts revolved round and round in her mind like a squirrel in a cage. What about the situation from David's point of view? Maybe, although he had asked her for a date, he too thought she was making a play for him, interested because of his money and position, keen for a home and all that his money could bring . . . surely he wasn't like that . . . and yet did she really know him after such a brief encounter? He's only a man after all, she thought with a trace of bitterness . . . what was it that girl had said? 'A slice off a cut loaf . . . ' was that the way he thought of her? She felt sick at the thought, at the implication . . . for a moment she thought of cancelling their date . . . but she felt too exhausted even to give an explanation, to work out a plausible lie . . . and she couldn't tell him the truth — mostly because she couldn't bear to see the look in his eyes in case what the girls had said — what she had begun to let herself suspect — might be true . . . somehow she would have to go through with the evening, to try and behave normally, to give herself time to think.

The girl who lived in the flat underneath Alison had promised to come and sit with Susi, she was saving up to get married, and 50p for an evening's baby sitting was appealing. She arrived just as Alison was pinning her hair on top of her head. Somehow she felt it would give her an older look, and she would be able to adopt a more coolly detached air than if she left it loose on her shoulders.

'You look super, Ali, only thing is it makes you seem older, more mature perhaps — and I love the colours in the dress, brings out the blue in your eyes.'

Alison forced a smile, she hardly cared really what she did look like . . . 'You sound quite poetic, Jean. Actually to be down to earth, there's a split in the skirt, which I've mended, I hope it doesn't show. Anyway we're only going to a country pub on the moor so I didn't think I'd wear my long skirt . . . '

'You look ever so nice. I've never known you go out with a bloke before, only the girls from the office, and then not often . . . do you good it will. Is he from Beresford's?'

Alison nodded. Although Jean knew all about the kidnapping, she wasn't particularly familiar with the Beresford set up, she taught in a village school a little way out of Ashleigh, and it was hardly likely she would know him. Alison felt she couldn't bear any more remarks, even if well meant, about her relationship with the boss . . .

The bell rang and Susi dashed to open the door. Alison had told her her beloved Uncle David was coming, and she had gone wild with delight, brushing Huggy Bear's fur, putting on his boiler suit Alison had made from some odd scraps of denim, almost too excited to eat her supper, until her mother had snapped at her and she'd looked up with surprise and hurt at the unusual tone, and Alison had quickly put her arms round her and said, 'Sorry love, I'm a bit tired . . . reaction I expect . . . '

David had on a thin wool shirt with a cravat and the dark linen trousers he'd worn at the house. He gave Alison a warm smile and took both her hands in his, 'You look enchanting, like a fresh spring breeze on this rather humid evening . . . '

She felt a physical shock as he touched her and her knees trembled, she turned quickly and said, 'This is Jean Fletcher, she lives in the flat underneath. She's going to keep an eye on Susi . . . '

He turned and gave Jean a courteous smile, and then bent down and picked up the child, 'And how's my best girl, eh? and that fabulous bear . . . ' She snuggled into his neck, Huggy Bear once more forgotten on the floor. He carried her over to the bed in the corner as she said, 'A story please, Uncle David. How is Helpful Rabbit and what is he going to be doing tonight?'

David started to tell her a story. Alison went through into the tiny kitchen and made some coffee and sandwiches for Jean, who was listening to David, almost as enthralled as Susi . . .

Now the moment had come, Alison felt an overwhelming nervousness at being alone with David — something she hadn't experienced the whole time she'd been at Woodrising. Then life had been complicated by Susi's kidnapping, but as far as their personal relationship was concerned she felt a natural kind of ease with him. But the overheard conversation had destroyed that feeling now . . .

It took some time to settle Susi down. Eventually Alison kissed her and picked up Huggy Bear from the floor, giving Jean last minute instructions about how to contact her if anything should go wrong. David wrote down the phone number of the pub and she could see Jean gazing at him, thinking probably that he was old enough to be her father, realising he was a rich man from his gold pen to the expensive suede shoes . . . and once more she couldn't bear to think of the criticisms she might be making . . .

David had his damaged car back now. It smelt of real leather and expensive after shave and rich comfort. The cassette player gave out soft, romantic piano music, but she could only feel a deep bitterness, unable to enjoy it because of the words that kept going round and round in her mind . . .

Once or twice he turned his head and looked at her, surprised at her silence. She gazed fixedly at the road ahead, the tarmac shimmering in the heat of the evening, fingering the square edges of the envelope in the pocket of her dress. She had written the letter while she waited for Jean to arrive, saying things she couldn't put into words to his face.

Her head throbbed with a dull pain behind the eyes, she had a tight feeling in her chest almost as if she were sickening for some illness . . . how to get through the evening without breaking down, without all she felt bursting out like an undamned flood . . .

Her flesh shrank as he rested his hand lightly on her knee.

'Are you all right, Alison? You seem so quiet, reaction I expect. Perhaps you ought to let the doctor run the rule over you. You have borne up so wonderfully that there has to be a period of let down, like a delayed shock.'

She shook her head, unable to speak for a moment, afraid she would break down and sob out her feelings . . .

Eventually she said slowly 'I'm all right really, a bit tired, that's all. We've been fairly busy at the office. But I don't mean to seem ungrateful, I'm sorry I'm not very lively company.'

He put his hand back on the steering wheel. 'That's O.K. then, understandable you should feel exhausted. I don't suppose you slept much, even last night, and sleeping tablets don't give one the same kind of rest as old Mother Nature.'

She gazed at the passing scenery, the beauty of the open moors, the distant tors in the clear evening sunlight, a lark spiralled upwards into the upturned bowl of azure . . .

The pub stood on the edge of a moorland village, its garden sloping down to where a stream tumbled and chattered over moss covered stones. Small birds flew from rock to rock, twittering and fussing — for a moment they reminded her of the gossiping girls at the office.

There was a cobbled courtyard outside the dining room where a table had been set for two with candles in deep glass holders, and roses and wisteria tumbled and twined above their heads on a trellis so that the evening sky was only seen in patches and they appeared to be in a cool green cave.

Afterwards she could scarcely remember what they ate, although it had been a fabulous meal . . . a salad of fresh salmon from the Dart, strawberries and thick yellow cream, coffee, and the luxurious taste of good brandy on her tongue. But all the time as she tried to meet his eyes in the candlelight, the faces of the girls rose before her, dancing, mocking, teasing — mouthing the words . . . 'Isn't she lucky to have hooked D.B.?'

She realised he had said something to which she should have replied. He was looking at her quizzically through the blue haze of cigar smoke.

'Sorry, I shouldn't be chattering about my troubles, but really Sara has been playing me up as if she was Jo-Anne's age these last few days. I don't know what's the matter with her, now she says she wants to get out of Woodrising, to have her own place. A flat in London if you please. I expect in the end I shall have to let her for the sake of peace. In which case it would be pointless to keep the house on in Ashleigh. It's much too big . . . and I shall miss Jo-Anne dreadfully.'

She felt a deep momentary pity for him. He looked almost stricken. Then, unbidden, into her mind sprang the thought . . . 'Maybe Sara thinks I'm after her father too . . . she probably thinks I'm doing all right and wants a place of her own before I take over . . . '

She turned the brandy glass round and round, watching the candlelight as it caught the tawny liquid in its flame, wondering why life had always to turn out sour, bitter . . . then feeling he expected some kind of comment from her, she said slowly, 'But what about her husband's job — I mean he works at the Ashleigh factory doesn't he?'

He nodded, 'Yes, but as you know, we have a London branch, I suppose I could put him in charge up there, but it means moving the present man, and more work for me this end. I was hoping for the contrary, hoping to have a little more leisure to enjoy myself,' he glanced at her, then added 'oh dear, I wonder why people have to complicate life so much . . . '

Now he watched the candlelight as it played on the planes and angles of her face — beautiful bone structure, the kind of face that would get even more beautiful in fact as she grew older. Like Joy's had been. No wonder artists had wanted to paint her. This girl wasn't much older than she had been when she died. Now it all seemed so long ago, in another life almost . . . this was little more than a child that sat the other side of the polished table . . . a child whom it was difficult to believe was herself a mother, and he old enough to be her father . . . He sighed. He was irresistibly drawn to this girl with whom he had suffered so much in a comparatively short time. And he knew now it was a great deal more than pity he felt for her, and pity was akin to love . . . but what right had he to think of her with the thoughts of a lover? What could she possibly see in him. What chance had he against a younger man, and for all he knew she probably already had a lover, although she had never spoken of anyone, never cried out their name in her anguish. But there had been dozens of cases where a girl had been half the age of her husband, and it had worked . . . but somehow Alison had a freedom of manner, of spirit, an independence far beyond her years. She would probably want a man her equal in years. She had indeed clung to him over the past hours in her need — but it was the kind of need that rarely occurred more than once in a life time. Her resources must have been stretched to their limit. Anyone who could help, who could be leaned upon, would naturally have been welcome.

Maybe this would have to be sufficient. The idea filled him with a deep sadness, a feeling of utter depression, caught from her own mood perhaps

He got up slowly, 'Would you like to go home? I know it's early yet, but I'm sure you need a good night's sleep.'

She glanced at her watch. It was only a little after ten but she wouldn't have been surprised if it were midnight. She was acutely conscious she had spoiled his evening, been a wet blanket, but there was nothing she could do about it. If only she hadn't heard the words those wretched girls had said at least until after their date. She was more than ever in his debt now.

She followed him out to the car park, feeling the crackle of the letter in her pocket. She knew that would cause him even more sorrow, but she was only

trying to do the thing she thought best
. . . that she would regret the decision
she knew was possible, but on the face
of it she couldn't think of any other way
out . . . at least she had Susi . . . she
would be no worse off than she had
been before the kidnapping happened,
before David came into her life . . .

They drove home in silence, the wonder
of the after-glow all about them, a scarlet sky shot with gold and saffron, fading
to palest primrose and blue where a
single star hung like a newly lighted
lamp, and across the whole, like a splash
from an artist's brush a crimson vapour
trail from a jet plane, catching the rays
of the hidden sun — enough beauty to
fill the heart . . . beauty that cried out to
be shared . . . but neither of them spoke
or remarked on it, each sensing that
something, some barrier had arisen between
them.

He drew up outside the flat slowly,
reluctant to let her go. 'You wouldn't
like to come back to Woodrising just for
a coffee or a night cap?' He turned to

look at her profile, pale in the thickening dusk. 'I've got the record of the music for the Snow Goose, and it really is beautiful. I thought we'd let Susi hear it some time. Does she know the story by Paul Gallico?'

She shook her head slowly, catching her breath on a sob, thinking of what might have been, what could have been . . . then without actually answering, she drew the letter from her pocket, her other hand already on the door catch so she could escape as soon as she had given it to him . . .

'I wrote you this,' he could hardly hear the words, her head bowed. He took it reluctantly half aware of what it might contain, and yet unable to believe it, holding it by one corner as if it might burn his flesh. She opened the door and swung her legs to the pavement before he could make any move to prevent her. 'Goodbye, and thank you again, for everything . . . '

He put out his hand to touch her 'Just a moment. Why the letter Alison?

I'll see you at the office, or we'll have another evening out, when you're less tired,' he paused a moment, keeping his tone light, grinning crookedly at her half turned head 'and there are lots more instalments about Helpful Rabbit . . . surely . . . '

She slid away from him, her upswept hair catching in the top of the door in her haste so that some of the pins fell out and a strand of silky hair hung round her face. 'No, I'm sorry, you'll see when you read it . . . I've given in my resignation at the office . . . '

Before what she had said could sink in, she'd gone, running swiftly up the steps, banging the door behind her with a finality that echoed through his mind and heart . . . For a moment he moved as if to go after her . . . but he knew she meant it . . . there was nothing he could do, nothing but wait and hope that whatever had upset her would resolve itself, for he knew now that without her life would be an empty and untenable existence . . .

12

The days that followed took on a dream quality. Alison felt as if she were being torn into two — one part of her cried out to stay, to let everything go on as before — no, not as before, that could never be now, her relationship with David had inevitably altered — but at least the life she was used to . . .

The other half urged her to make a clean break, to get away and start a new life somewhere else. After all, what had she to keep her in Ashleigh now? Friends, perhaps, but none close enough to matter, she could make fresh ones elsewhere . . .

She knew she was running away from herself as much as from the situation, and yet in her heart she was certain that this was really something no one could do . . .

Partly perhaps it was the problem of

coming to terms with the idea of having a man in her life again, she had been alone, self sufficient and independent for so long — it would mean a complete reassessment of her whole outlook, her attitude, to have to think of another person's feelings, opinions and wishes would be strange, in a way independence was a precious commodity . . . and yet in the long watches of the night she longed for someone to lean on as she had on David for those few short hours. But then, as the cold light of day penetrated the shabby curtains, she knew she couldn't face the gossip and talk . . . a nine days' wonder it might be, but she wouldn't be able to take the looks in their eyes, the unspoken criticism, the barely concealed salacious innuendoes.

But where to go? What to do? She had little choice for it wouldn't be easy to find somewhere to live even, with a small girl, and she had no intention of sending Susi to a boarding school of any kind, anyhow such an idea would be far beyond her means.

It felt strange the next day not to go to the office as usual. She'd rung up Miss Atwood and told her she was sorry but owing to domestic difficulties she had had to tender her resignation to Personnel, she hoped she would understand and not be put to too much inconvenience . . . Miss Atwood had been non-committal, but not as angry as Alison had feared. Maybe she too recognised the atmosphere her presence created and felt it unwelcome . . .

Later she went to pick Susi up from Playschool. She'd bought the local papers and scanned them for a job. Exeter or Plymouth would be sufficiently far away and impersonal — she couldn't bear the idea of leaving Devon entirely, and she would be able to lose herself in the anonymity of either city.

She marked one or two — an advertisement for a housekeeper to a widower with two small children where another child would not be objected to . . . at least that would mean a roof over her head and that Susi could be with her . . . housework and cooking were something she could do . . .

There was another for a gardener and driver to an elderly lady . . . either sex, no nursing or lifting, must be a dog lover . . . Alison had a momentary vision of a snapping poodle or snuffling pekinese — and although there was no mention of it, felt sure a child would not be welcome . . . she drafted out an advertisement of her own for a job similar to the first one. She didn't altogether relish the idea of being a housekeeper, housework was not among her favourite jobs, it was bound to be a pretty humdrum existence, on top of which she would, in someone else's house, be sacrificing her privacy . . . but in the crazy mixed up state she found herself, she had little choice.

As she drew into the kerb outside the Playschool a voice called, 'Hi there Mrs. Ross. Nice to see you again . . . '

She looked round in surprise for the voice seemed vaguely familiar, but for the moment she couldn't place the owner . . . then she saw the Sergeant — Mitchell — or Mitch as everyone called him, the one who had been on the case looking for Susi . . . she smiled. He was a nice guy . . .

'Hi yourself. On another case are you?'

He shook his head, 'No, as a matter of fact my boy Stevie goes here to Playschool, but I don't generally manage to pick him up, my next door neighbour does it for me, that's why we haven't met here before,' he gave a friendly grin, 'but I've got a spot of leave and thought I'd pop down to fetch him . . .'

'I didn't realise he was at the same place as Susi . . .' she said.

'I don't suppose you did. Actually it's his last term. How about your Susi — is she off to a new school as well next term?'

Alison looked away for a moment as the colour flooded her face. Then she turned and said with a touch of defiance, 'She is leaving, yes . . . as a matter of fact we both are — leaving Ashleigh I mean . . . '

For a moment a look of disappointment wiped the grin from his face, then he said quickly, 'I hope you're not deserting us altogether as a result of the unfortunate experience you had — not going too far away I mean . . . '

'I . . .' she hesitated. It occurred to her that as a policeman he might just possibly have some knowledge of the kind of job she wanted . . . 'as a matter of fact I'm going to make a break, find another job if I can . . . '

He glanced at her swiftly, his gaze penetrating, then he said, 'A pity, still, while you are here, how about coming out for a drink and a snack tonight? That is, crime permitting of course.' He grinned again and she thought what a nice friendly person he was. She did feel a kind of acute loneliness, desolation almost, but she wasn't sure if Mitch's company was the solution, nice as he seemed to be . . . she realised as she thought about it that he must have known Susi was at the same school as Stevie, and that probably she would come to pick her up . . . as she remembered how kind he'd been during those terrible hours, different altogether from the rather austere Inspector — she wondered if perhaps he'd been interested in her then . . . he had told her his wife was dead, they had much in common in a way for it couldn't be any easier for a man to bring up a child on his own than it was for her with Susi . . .

She realised he was waiting for her answer. 'Yes, thank you, I'd like that, but I really can't ask my next door neighbour to baby sit again . . . ' she hesitated, unwilling in the light of recent happenings to tell him she'd been out with David — her boss . . .

'That's no problem. We can leave her at my place, I have a most reliable old dear who will come when I'm on duty and so on, she'll be quite O.K. in the spare room . . . '

He made it all sound so easy . . . and she needed someone to talk to, someone disinterested who could give her advice perhaps, help to sort out her confused thoughts . . .

It was such a contrast to her night out with David. Mitch lived in a semi on a new estate not far from Exeter. The house had the rather uncared for, bleak atmosphere that indicates the lack of a woman's touch. Stevie was a nice little boy, but she remembered Susi had told her he was one of the chief mischief makers at school. Now she realised it was probably because Mitch, at home, bent over backwards to be strict with him, and she noticed he picked on him constantly over small things . . . it was no wonder he played up at school.

'I live away from Ashleigh,' Mitch told her, 'because I used to be stationed at the nick in this area and I didn't particularly want to move, although I bring Stevie over to Playschool because now I'm stationed in Ashleigh. I know it all sounds rather complicated, but it works out quite well . . . '

Mrs. Mack, the baby sitter arrived. She was a rotund little person reminding Alison of a wooden doll she'd had as a child, weighted at the bottom so you couldn't knock it over . . . she felt sure Mrs. Mack was as stolid. She was carrying numerous shopping bags which bulged with knitting, balls of wool, slippers, a bottle of orange squash and other odds and ends . . . but her presence created an aura of confidence so that she felt quite happy at leaving Susi in her care.

They had a beer at a bright new pub out on the bypass, and scampi in a basket. Mitch was easy to talk to . . . Alison told him she felt things had changed since the kidnapping — many things . . .

His eyes twinkled as she spoke, 'I know, they think you're making a pass at the boss, and vice versa . . . '

She looked up quickly, ridiculously and unreasonably hurt at his tone

. . . but there was no malice in his expression . . .

'How on earth did you know?'

'Usual and obvious in the kind of circumstances. I wouldn't let it throw you though . . . '

'Oh it's easy for you to say that,' she sighed 'I really feel it would be better to go away, make a clean break . . . '

He too was serious now as he looked at her. He took her hand in both his, 'I need someone to look after Stevie — and me . . . how about taking it on? Purely as a business proposition of course,' he added, seeing the expression of caution on her face.

She withdrew her hand gently, 'It's very kind of you, but really that wouldn't solve anything would it?'

He nodded ruefully, 'I suppose as soon as I'd thought of it I realised it was too good an idea to work . . . still, at least will you sleep on it? Think it over for a day or two. I don't imagine you're in all that much of a hurry to get away.'

'I am actually. Although I've got a

little bit of money in the bank for a rainy day, I don't want to use it unless it's for something really desperate . . . '

She was instantly relieved that he didn't offer to lend her money, she couldn't have borne that . . .

'I don't really see that it wouldn't solve your problem at least for the moment,' he said slowly 'the house is after all some miles from Ashleigh, it's a suburb of Exeter, and it's hardly likely you'd see anyone from here . . . you'd do all your shopping and so on in Exeter and there's a good bus service . . . I'd take Susi to Playschool with Stevie till they go to Primary . . . there's a good one close by . . . '

She smiled. 'You sound like an estate agent!'

He grinned back. 'More important than selling a house, I'm trying to sell Stevie and myself . . . ' He got to his feet, 'one for the road, then we'll go, I'm sure you must be tired, and I have to run Mrs. Mack home . . . '

As they drove along the darkened

lanes he said, 'I've enjoyed this evening so much, more than I've enjoyed anything for a long time. You're a very sympathetic person to be with — you know that?'

'Thank you, and you're a very kind one,' she said softly.

'Not kind,' he corrected. 'I can imagine what you've been through and I know what hell it must have been — losing someone is as though the world has come to an end, and you came very near to it . . .'

As he spoke she realised what a lonely life he must lead. Maybe because she felt fate had been good to her in returning Susi unharmed, she felt at least she owed something in return . . . maybe bringing a bit of happiness and comfort to this man and his child could be a kind of repayment . . . it was crazy reasoning, it wouldn't repay David for all he'd done, and she knew in a way she'd treated him badly, but she was so mixed up, so confused . . .

She had a restless night, tossing and

turning, trying to sort out her tangled thoughts . . . but by morning she had come to a decision — if Susi would accept the idea of living in the same house as Mitch and Stevie — of her mother being home instead of in an office — and if, hardest of all — she could explain that they wouldn't be seeing Uncle David any more . . . then she would accept Mitch's offer . . .

She was heavy eyed at breakfast. Susi was quiet as if she sensed that her mother had something on her mind. But at last, pouring fresh orange juice into their glasses, Alison said —

'Susi, you know I've given in my notice at the office, that I had thought we would make a move, and this is as good a time as any as you have to go to a new school next term . . . '

Susi put down her spoon — she had been about to feed Huggy Bear with his share of cornflakes . . . she nodded . . .

'Yes — but it'll mean we have to go away from Uncle David won't it?' Her candid blue eyes looked directly into

Alison's. She knew there was much more going on in the child's mind than she could possibly fathom at the moment ... 'I sort of love Uncle David,' the child said softly ... Alison looked away quickly before the sob in her throat should escape through her lips ... then she said slowly, 'There are some things that little girls, even little girls as wise as you, can't understand darling, you'll just have to trust me ... and you do like Stevie don't you? I mean you get on well at school?'

'Oh yes, he's alright, as far as boys go,' she said now, offering Huggy his orange juice, 'but what's that got to do with it?'

Alison explained Mitch's offer. 'It's a nice house, much more room than here, you'd be able to have your own room, and there's a garden with a swing and a sand pit ... and a kind of patio place to have a barbecue ... '

Susi rested her chin on her hand, her eyes wise ... 'That's not really why we're going though is it Mummy?'

Alison got to her feet quickly, 'I didn't say we were definitely going, love, if you hate the idea . . . ' she knew she'd avoided a direct reply to the child's question.

Susi slipped from her chair and went over to her mother, putting her soft arms round her neck and resting her cheek against her hair.

'I don't mind . . . but Huggy's going to miss Uncle David too, and we'll never hear the end of that story about H.R.,' she paused, 'still, at least I'll be with you more won't I? And you won't have to go to that horrid old office . . . the holidays will be fun, and I 'spect between the two of us women we can manage those two men . . . ' she gave a rather tremulous smile as she looked up at her mother, Alison stooped down, squatting on her heels, and said shakily . . . 'Thank you for being so understanding love . . . '

Mitch was like a dog with two tails when Alison saw him later at Playschool . . . 'How soon can I pick you up?'

'I haven't much to pack, can you arrange for some kind of van to take the bits of furniture? You wouldn't mind my bringing it would you, there are just our beds and one or two odds and ends . . .'

'Of course, bring anything you want to,' he said jubilantly, 'I'll arrange for a pal of mine to come round this afternoon, then you can come home with us this evening when you pick Susi up . . .'

It all seemed to have happened so quickly, and she still didn't know if she'd made the right decision, but at least she had made one, and she supposed in her present state of mind that was something.

As she packed up their things at the flat she stood taking a last look round, remembering how she had trailed the streets picking up bits and pieces from secondhand shops . . . and somehow although he'd only been there a couple of times, she kept thinking of David as he sat on Susi's bed, telling her a bedtime story . . .

13

Alison found that Mitch's house needed more than just a woman's touch. It had become sadly neglected.

She washed covers and curtains and painted where she could. The brass had lost its lustre and the garden was overgrown.

Mitch seemed to work all hours with no particular routine, he didn't even have regular time off, and she realised how much Stevie must have been left to neighbours and Mrs. Mack . . .

It was a nice enough little house but with no personality. As for Stevie, he seemed as pleased with the new régime as his father, and secretly Alison couldn't help being amused at the rather proprietary attitude Susi adopted with him — there was no question who was going to rule this particular household, and fortunately the two menfolk seemed to accept it quite happily. Even on Sundays Mitch was on call if an emergency arose — and sometimes even if it didn't.

'Don't you ever get a holiday?' Alison protested, 'or any proper time off?'

He smiled ruefully, 'I suppose I could get more if I asked,' he looked away for a moment, 'but sometimes the hours have dragged, even with Stevie . . . and work is a great panacea . . . '

'I know,' she said quickly, 'but now I'm here . . . ' she broke off, not sure of what she had been going to suggest . . .

He glanced at her, and for a moment she read something more than interest — admiration in his eyes, and she looked away, changing the subject, uncertain of her feelings . . .

After supper she said, 'Come out into the garden, it's still as hot as midday, and I want you to show me how to prune the roses, they have got terribly overgrown, and some of the blooms are beautiful.'

He got a rusty pair of secateurs from

the kitchen drawer, and rolling up his sleeves, said, 'It isn't really the right time of year, the only thing one can do is cut off the dead heads and some of the weaker growth . . . ' When he'd finished she picked a big bunch of the buds and full grown roses and put them in a vase on the kitchen table, the perfume filling the sun drenched room.

Mitch was tinkering with the mowing machine as if her encouragement had inspired him to help tidy up. Soon the summer smell of fresh cut grass wafted through the open window as he ran the machine over the lush growth . . .

She stood watching him. He wasn't exactly good looking, nothing like David, but he had a nice face and a slim, lithe figure . . . she knew he liked sport and had excelled at school for there was a cupboard filled with silver cups — also sadly neglected. When she mentioned the fact to him he said ruefully, 'I'd like to take up golf, but any spare time I have I've spent with Stevie of course . . . '

'Well there's nothing to stop you now,' she said, and for a moment he'd looked as if he were about to say something and then changed his mind . . .

Occasionally Mrs. Mack came in to sit with the children so that Mitch and Alison could go out for a meal, but, like a doctor, wherever he went he had to leave his telephone number, and more often than not he was called back to some incident or other . . .

'No wonder they say crime is on the increase,' she said rather ruefully one evening just as the prawn cocktail had been brought at the start of their meal, and he was called to the phone.

'I'll have to go, they've fished some poor old geyser out of the river at Ashleigh . . . '

She sighed with resignation.

'You stay and finish your dinner,' he said. But she shook her head.

'I never did like eating alone, and anyway it would mean a taxi home, and you'll need something when you eventually get home . . . '

He shrugged smiling, 'No wonder they wrote a song which said a policeman's lot is not a happy one!' For a moment he looked serious, once again as if something was on the tip of his tongue, then he picked up his jacket. 'Well perhaps your suggestion would be best, with all the crime and violence there is about I don't fancy leaving such a pretty girl on her own!'

When Alison went into the lounge, Mrs. Mack was sitting with her eyes glued to the television. 'Would you like Mr. Mitchell to run you home now?' she asked.

'I'll stay and keep you company — and I want to see the end of the film,' she said, indicating the galloping horses with her knitting needle. Mitch winked at Alison in the doorway, it was an endless source of amusement to him that the old lady was a Western addict . . . 'I think that John Wayne's just lovely,' she often said . . .

Mitch drove off and Alison went into the kitchen to make coffee. 'Have the children been good?' she asked as she brought in the tray.

'Like little lambs, never a sound,' the old woman said as the film ended with a burst of gunfire and the two goodies rode off into the sun baked, cactus strewn desert . . . she finished the row she was knitting and then wrapped the completed work round the needles. As she sipped her coffee she looked at Alison with shrewd eyes.

'Mind if I say something personal, Mrs. Ross? I'm not given to gossip, but I'm very fond of Mr. Mitchell and young Stevie, known them since his poor Mum died, lovely girl she was, terrible sad thing for a young couple . . . still, 'tisn't that I was going to mention . . .'

Alison looked at her in surprise, nice as she was, she was a woman of few words normally . . . 'Of course, feel free to say anything you like, I can assure you I won't be offended, and neither

224

will I repeat anything you say to me in confidence, of course . . . '

'Well, 'tis that Mrs. Merritt at number ten, always had her eye on Mr. Mitchell,' she paused and gave a sniff, 'nice enough young person I daresay, but not good enough for him, though I daresay 'tis none of her fault her husband left her — 'cepting I say usually 'tis six of one and half a dozen of another . . . '

Alison wondered what on earth all this was leading up to and wished she would come to the point . . .

'Personally, myself, I think you're doing a grand job here, made the house ever so nice, and Mr. Mitchell is a different person since you been here, but even in these days of what they call the permissive society and all that, some people like to make trouble . . . '

'You mean she thinks it's not right for me to live here and not be married to Mr. Mitchell?' Alison said quickly . . .

'Something like that — mind, I know

there's no hanky panky, I'd soon know, and any road 'tisn't anyone else's business, I say, what you do, but it's young Stevie and your Susi I'm thinking 'bout. When they goes to Primary next year, there's lots of kids from the estate go there, and you know what people are, specially about the police, any chance they can find something wrong they will . . . just for the devil of it . . . '

Once more the suffocating feeling of horror filled Alison . . . at the idea people were gossiping, pointing fingers at her . . . she had thought that here at least she would be free of all that . . . had never really imagined anyone could find any fault . . . how wrong she had been . . .

Mrs. Mack went rumbling on. Alison hardly heard what she said . . . and then there was the sound of Mitch's car in the drive, and the old women got to her feet . . . 'Now don't you take any notice of what they say m'dear, they won't dare tell me their nasty ideas to my face

226

or they'll get the edge of my tongue
. . . tongue pie my husband used to call
it . . . but I thought you ought to
know . . . '

For a moment Alison felt like
running upstairs like a child and
burying her face in the bedclothes,
sobbing out the misery that once more
filled her . . . or pouring out all she had
heard to Mitch . . . but she knew that
would be unfair, immature . . . that
kind of gossip had to be ignored, she
couldn't spend the rest of her life
running . . . running . . . but again she
felt the bitter poison of the innuendo,
imagined pointing fingers of suspicion
and knew that now each time she went
out of the house, got into the car,
shopped in the local supermarket, she
would feel sure everyone was talking
behind her back . . . one or two of the
other women had admittedly made half
hearted attempts to be friendly, but she
had felt they were wary of something
— Mitch being a policeman perhaps —
now she was certain it was of her and

the position she was in . . .

If Mitch noticed her preoccupation over the next few days, he didn't remark on it. But one evening after working in the garden, they sat over a late cup of coffee in the kitchen and she felt she had to bring up the subject that weighed increasingly on her mind. Not looking at him, her eyes lowered, she said slowly.

'Mitch, aren't people going to talk — I mean about me living here like this . . . ' she felt the colour suffusing her face as she spoke . . .

She felt him give her a swift look, and then he said firmly, 'As my superiors at the nick know about it and have no objections, it really doesn't matter a tinker's cuss to me what anyone else thinks . . . ' then he added ruefully, 'You get used to that in the force, once a policeman always a policeman they say, fuzz is one of the better names we get called . . . '

'I know all that,' she looked up at him now, 'but it does matter to me . . . and perhaps Stevie and Susi . . . '

He came over and took her hand quickly, 'I'm sorry, I hadn't realised, how very stupid and thoughtless of me . . . ' He sat down and released her fingers . . . for a moment he said nothing, then he got up again and went over to the sink, picking up their cups from the draining board and starting to rinse them as if he needed something to occupy his hands . . .

'I know this isn't really the time or place, and I didn't intend to speak of it so soon, I realise we haven't known each other for long, but sometimes it doesn't take long,' he hesitated and suddenly she knew clearly what was coming, but the words she longed to say to stop him wouldn't form themselves on her stiff lips, and she let him continue . . .

'You and I have quite a lot in common, we've both . . . well . . . lost the one person in the world for us . . . '

She caught her breath . . . did he mean the nebulous Johnnie of whom she had told him briefly, thinking it unfair not to . . . or did he mean David, who had never been hers, and now never would be . . . Mitch went on speaking . . .

'Don't you think we might find — consolation, companionship . . . on a permanent and perhaps more conventional basis?' He turned round now, his hair standing endearingly on end where he had run his fingers through it, he hardly looked any older than Stevie, his eyes appealing . . . 'I'm making an awful mess of this, I'd probably find it much easier to write down as a report!' he grinned tremulously, and for some ridiculous reason she wanted to cry . . . and yet a kind of numbness surrounded her heart. 'You're asking me to marry you?' she hardly recognised her own voice, the words came out in a kind of flat, tonelessness . . .

'I'm sorry I put it so clumsily . . . I do hope I haven't offended you.' He was distressed, contrite . . . he knew from her tone, from the expression on her face what the answer would be . . . 'I was a fool ever to ask, even to expect . . .'

'I'm sorry too,' her voice was hardly above a whisper, 'but companionship, consolation . . . somehow they don't mean marriage to me . . . perhaps I'm incurably romantic, asking too much, heaven knows I should have learnt better I suppose, but I do want love, real love . . .'

He moved towards her, his hands outstretched, almost as if in supplication . . . 'That's what I'm offering you. I think I loved you from that very first moment, in Beresford's office when you were describing Susi . . . of course then I knew nothing about you, whether you had a husband or not, I just thought, 'here is a girl I could love for always, could marry' . . . there wasn't any rhyme or reason to it. As a matter of fact before I saw you I'd have been the very last person even to acknowledge such a thing could happen. In the past I've ridiculed such a thing in other people

. . . it's just something I can't explain . . . '

She put her hand on his arm . . . 'It wouldn't be any good pretending . . . for me I mean . . . it wouldn't be fair on you or Stevie or Susi . . . or me, on any of us . . . '

He looked like a dog that had been kicked by the one it adored. 'No, I know I was blinded by it and felt sure it must be returned it was so overwhelming, I just hoped, because my own love was so strong . . . is so strong . . . I realise I've made a complete fool of myself . . . please forgive me . . . '

Let me say the right thing, she prayed, let whatever words I use put the whole thing into its proper perspective, please let it be right, don't let me hurt him. Because he had said what he had, now with a blinding clarity she realised if she loved again, if she ever married it would have to be David . . . it could never be anyone else . . . the idea of being anyone else's wife was quite untenable.

Now she felt his eyes on her again.

232

'There just isn't anything to forgive, for one thing there's no greater compliment anyone can receive than a proposal of marriage,' she paused, and then with an attempt at lightness, 'not that I even let you actually get the words out! I rather jumped the gun didn't I?'

Now he managed a smile, some of the tension eased. 'You're the most extraordinary person,' he sighed and turned away, picking up a paint brush she had been using earlier and starting to clean it off on a sheet of newspaper. Then he said without turning round, 'This doesn't mean I've scared you off does it? That you'll try to find another job, go away just when Stevie and I are getting used to being spoiled, really starting to live . . . '

She shook her head slowly. 'Not if you want me to stay, but I think it must be on a temporary basis as we agreed at first . . . on both sides I mean . . . if you . . . '

'If I don't force myself on you,' he

broke in, turning round and looking at her with a quizzical expression on his face. 'I promise to behave . . . but I won't promise it'll be easy . . .'

And so the weeks went by. Alison and Susi had settled into a routine, a pleasant routine she had to admit. Mitch kept his word and never mentioned his proposal. He was so kind, so gentle with the children, treating Susi exactly the same way as Stevie so that sometimes it was even possible to imagine they really were a complete family . . .

When he had a few hours off they would go out in the car with a picnic meal and go to the beach or the moor where Mitch was teaching Stevie to fish in the river. Even Susi had her own rod and line as she seemed to want to do everything Stevie did . . . and the boy was gentle with her and never jealous . . . It had developed into an uncomplicated and comfortable relationship and she looked forward to the rare evenings they spent together when the telephone didn't interrupt them, they would sit and listen to records, talking, or sometimes just sitting. Now she had convinced herself it was an ordinary man girl relationship — but sometimes she even thought it might be easy, the solution, to fall in love with him . . . as he had said, they had much in common, a love of music, of good food, of the beauty of the Devon countryside — and then there were the children . . . and yet again she couldn't really imagine their future together, and often, with a feeling of guilt, she longed for David with every fibre of her being, just to hear his voice, to feel the touch of his hand, and she wondered if she had thrown away the chance of a lifetime of happiness through foolishness, a kind of pride, because in her heart she had known her love for him was real and she had become even more convinced of this since she had been away from him . . . Sometimes she felt such a rush of emotion and longing she hardly knew how to bear it

. . . when she was out shopping, or going to the moor or beach with Mitch she would see the signpost to Ashleigh, or the boards with initials HR about which David had made up the charming stories for Susi, and her heart felt as though it couldn't stand the ache for him . . . then she would recall the conversation she had overheard . . . and once more the poison filled her mind . . .

And then one evening when Mitch came home earlier than usual, she was in the garden where she was trying to spend more time now, burning up the weeds and rubbish from the flower beds . . . the air was filled with the smell of the coming autumn, although summer still lingered as if reluctant to leave the scorched fields and hedges . . . the children were having a last romp, pushing each other on the swing . . . voices came from nearby gardens, subtly different from the sounds of high summer — sharper, with an added clarity from the still air . . .

And directly she saw his face she knew he had something he was unwilling to tell her, but which had to be told . . .

14

Alison got to her feet from where she had been kneeling by the bonfire, realising from the expression on Mitch's face that he had something to tell her . . .

'Something's happened . . . ?'

He nodded, and then took both her hands in his, standing for a moment just looking at her, knowing in his heart that the news he had brought somehow was bad for him . . . perhaps unwelcome to her . . .

'The trial of the two kidnappers, it's next week . . . you'll have to go back to Ashleigh while it lasts . . . '

For a moment the world seemed to somersault. She had of course known she would have to be a witness for the prosecution, but somehow in the tranquillity of the past few weeks she had pushed it to the back of her mind

. . . there was so much else to do. Like a small child she had thought, if I don't think about it it'll go away, knowing all the time it could not be so . . . and yet in a way half longing to go back, to see David . . .

She put out her hand instinctively for support. He led her gently through the open door into the kitchen where she sank into a chair. He went into the lounge without speaking, and brought back the sherry, pouring them a glass each. Still she hadn't been able to speak . . .

'Here, try this on for size,' he said, trying to keep his tone light, and suddenly in the realisation of what he must be thinking, feeling, she forgot her own problems — she knew instinctively this was going to be the end for them . . . that once she was back, near David, whatever might transpire, she wouldn't be able to return to Mitch, although it seemed totally irrational to think thus, it was as if she were gazing into a crystal ball, it was as certain as if it had already happened . . . but in what way it would happen, what the ultimate outcome would be, she couldn't tell . . . only that everything would change once more . . .

Gratefully she sipped the drink he had poured, feeling its warmth run along the coldness of her limbs. In spite of the warmth of the late summer evening, a deadly chill seemed to have overcome her so she had difficulty in stopping her teeth from chattering . . .

'The period for which they had been remanded in custody ends of course with the trial . . . ' Mitch went on . . .

At that moment Susi came running in from the garden and hearing what he said asked, 'What's demanded in custard mean Mitch?'

The childish query broke the tension as they both laughed . . . 'Remanded in custody, darling, it means simply kept in prison . . . '

Susi had already lost interest in the grown up talk as she said to Mitch, 'You never came to see what we've built in the sand pit . . . '

He bent down and swung her up on to his shoulder, 'Never mind, I'll come in just a moment, I don't guess the tide'll come in and wash it away!'

She chuckled and snuggled up to him . . . 'course not silly . . . the sea's miles away . . . '

'How about you and Stevie going along to the shop and bringing some fish and chips for supper eh?' He put her down and pulled a note from his pocket . . .

'Oh super . . . wait till I tell Stevie, it's his favourite nosh . . . enough for you and Mummy too?'

He nodded. 'Yes, off you go . . . ' For a moment Susi glanced at her mother, seeing she was upset.

'Are you all right Mummy?' she came over and put her arm round her mother's neck.

Alison managed a smile. 'Of course, love, and no chips with mine, I'll get as fat as a pig . . . '

Susi kissed her on the cheek and skipped out of the door, shouting for

Stevie. Mitch was about to say . . . 'God knows they'll miss each other . . . ' but stopped short, persuading himself that perhaps he was wrong, that she would come back, maybe . . . he gave an involuntary shrug . . . that I should be so lucky . . . he murmured to himself.

Alison had composed herself now, they talked of arrangements of practical things . . .

'I don't know how long it'll take, it all depends, on the defence, on what other offences have to be taken into consideration — all kinds of things, but I shouldn't imagine more than a couple of days . . . but it would probably be best for you to stay in Ashleigh . . . ' his voice trailed off as he saw the expression on her face . . .

'Will you be staying too?'

He shook his head, 'I'll be around, but the Inspector will give the evidence for the C.I.D . . . '

'How about Susi . . . I don't want to take her into court if I can help it . . . '

'No, the statement she made is all

they will want . . . ' He turned away in case his face should show the emptiness that overwhelmed him at the thought of the house without her — without both of them for already he loved the little girl as if she were his own . . . 'I'll fix you a room at the local pub, then perhaps we can have dinner,' he smiled bleakly, and took her hand, 'Look, it isn't going to be easy for you I know, but I'll do everything I can . . . try not to worry too much . . . '

She held his hand to her cheek. 'You're so kind, much more than I deserve, I wish . . . '

He put the fingers of his other hand gently on her lips, outlining their curve, 'Don't say it . . . let's not either of us say anything we might regret, it's been so perfect . . . '

He turned away swiftly as if he didn't trust himself to say any more, and went out into the garden, picking up the fork where she had left it and pushing the sides of the bonfire into the middle so that sparks flew up in the gathering dusk . . .

Back in the kitchen Alison dropped her head on her arms and wept . . .

It was inevitable, as they drove to Ashleigh, that Susi should start to think about David . . .

'Will we be staying with Uncle David?'

'No darling, he did a lot for us when . . . ' even now she had difficulty in talking about those dark hours . . . 'when you were missing . . . we can't expect him to do any more for us . . . it's just that the Inspector will want to know all about what those men did . . . but it isn't anything for you to worry about, and Mitch will see to everything . . . '

Even as she reassured the child, she wondered how she was going to get through the next few days, with the kidnapping brought back vividly, those dark hours she had lived through, the inevitable meeting with David and the poignant memories he would evoke . . .

For some reason Ashleigh seemed smaller than she remembered it, even though she had gone for such a short while. The Golden Lion, where Mitch had booked them in, was a beautiful old pub with low beamed ceilings, chintz curtains and polished wood, brasses, and the smell of beer and cider mixed with beeswax and lavender. The early autumn day was cool and crisp beneath an intensely blue sky, and the log fire in the lounge was a welcome sight as they entered.

Susi ran to it, her hands outstretched . . . 'Look, Huggy, real logs, not those imitation kind like we've got at home.'

Mitch, who was carrying their cases, grinned at Alison, shrugging his shoulders in mock despair . . . he longed to say, 'At least she called my house home . . . ' but resisted the temptation . . . 'Don't push your luck, Mitchell,' he told himself.

Alison felt as if she were in some kind of vortex, a no man's land of indecision — what would she do when the trial was over she couldn't tell. Mitch was such a kind man, so good, she hated to take advantage of him indefinitely, knowing how they both felt, certain she could never return fully the love he had for her . . .

Last night as they drank their regular cup of coffee before bed, he had said briefly, 'I know I promised not to talk about it, but I do have to say this, Alison . . . there are different kinds of loving . . . ' The bewildered unhappiness in his voice tore at her heartstrings as she listened.

He went on softly, 'For some people there is the kind of love you spoke of, that you have obviously experienced, and I have too . . . maybe that is a lasting kind of loving, I don't know, neither of us had the chance to prove it . . . but I have always thought . . . hoped . . . that one day I would find the deep, steady, true kind . . . and I felt I had . . . ' She knew he was looking at her, but she couldn't lift her head.

'It isn't easy for me to talk like this . . . perhaps that's part of my trouble, maybe I should have ignored you asking me not to, should have told you more often what you mean to me . . . '

At last, her voice trembling, she said, 'I'm sorry Mitch, more sorry than I can possibly explain, but although I like you, respect you . . . perhaps as much or more than anyone I've ever known, I couldn't marry you . . . '

All night she had lain staring into the dark, bewildered, confused at her own feelings, and wishing one could love to order.

It was rather a silent drive and Alison felt relieved when they arrived in Ashleigh . . . Mrs. Barlow, the smiling owner of the pub, brought them tea and buttered toast, with cherry cake . . . Alison was very much aware that they must appear to be a complete and happy family . . .

Mitch tamped tobacco into his pipe, getting to his feet . . . 'I'll have to be getting along now, I'll be back in the morning to pick you both up and drive you to Court, I've arranged for a policewoman to look after Susi while you're actually in Court . . . you'll be O.K. till then the two of you?' His voice held a note of longing as his eyes sought hers . . . she turned her head, and he bent down and picked Susi up, holding her close for a moment. Then he put her down and turned abruptly, going out into the autumn evening, which seemed to be filled with a kind of poignant nostalgia which the end of summer brings . . . and felt as though he had left his heart behind him . . .

Alison unpacked their few belongings in the little bedroom under the eaves with its sloping roof and uneven walls. Susi sighed, 'It's a bit like our old flat isn't it? Cosy . . . I wonder what Stevie's doing, and what they'll have for supper, baked beans and beefburgers I bet, he said they lived on them before we went there . . . '

'Hurry up and get into bed, love,' Alison said a little more sharply than she had intended, but she found she'd come without their toothbrushes, which meant she'd have to go out, and she hated the idea of leaving Susi ... 'Don't leave the bedroom whatever you do, I'll tell Mrs. Barlow to pop up and see you're O.K., although I shouldn't be more than twenty minutes ... ' Leaving the door ajar she ran quickly down the stairs. Mrs. Barlow was in the bar getting ready for opening time, humming softly to herself.

'I shan't be a moment, I've left Susi getting ready for bed, it may be rather a long day for her tomorrow, if I'm more than a few minutes, would you mind popping up, or calling from the bottom of the stairs? I've left the door ajar.'

The woman smiled and nodded, 'Of course, I'll listen out for her, don't you worry, and I'll take her up some warm milk in a moment,' she paused, then went on, 'I can imagine how you feel about ever leaving her ... I thought at the time, when the kidnapping was on and all that, how terrible it must be for you, having brought up two of my own . . . ' she chattered on, meaning well, but Alison was anxious to get to the chemist before he closed . . . and she felt exhausted and ready for bed herself . . . not so much with the day passed as with the thoughts of the one to come and all it would entail, and perhaps the meeting with David most of all . . .

She hurried along the main street, past a flower shop where buckets of chyrsanthemums stood, their sharp smell filling the air. She gave a little shiver, winter would soon be here, some of the shops already had Christmas cards on display . . . Christmas . . . where would they be, she and Susi . . . she felt an acute pang of loneliness, almost of despair . . . but it was ridiculous, the feeling that she had no one . . . no one but Susi . . . and yet it was true, and her own fault, her own choice . . . the knowledge brought little comfort . . .

The chemist was full. The local

doctor was holding a surgery and many of his patients were waiting for prescriptions . . . she waited to be served with ill concealed impatience . . .

Then to her dismay out of the corner of her eyes she saw Miss Atwood . . . she tried to hide behind one of the stands that held soft drinks, but the woman had seen her. Her eyes lit up with curiosity as she came over.

'Hullo, Mrs. Ross. I thought I might see you around, I read the trial was coming off this week . . . ' she looked Alison up and down, . . . I wonder if she expects me to be showing signs of being pregnant,' Alison thought bitterly. 'How are things? Got another job have you? We haven't heard anything of you since you left . . . ' she paused, evidently hoping Alison would launch into a vivid description of all she had been doing . . . 'We don't see much of Mr. Beresford either,' she said pointedly, 'he spends a lot of time in London, his daughter and her husband have gone there to live, there's some talk of his selling Woodrising . . . ' she gave Alison a shrewd look, 'still I've no doubt you know all about that . . . '

Alison shook her head 'No, I didn't know. We live near Exeter now and I don't get over here at all . . . Susi goes to Primary school next term,' she said briefly, thankful that at that moment the assistant came to serve her, and to take Miss Attwood's prescription, which needed something explaining . . . Alison picked up her purchase and turning swiftly said . . . 'Goodbye, nice to have seen you . . . ' blushing at the lie.

However Miss Attwood didn't appear to notice and said, beaming, 'Do come to the office and have a chat, we'd all love to see dear little Susi again after her terrible ordeal . . . so glad it turned out so well in the end . . . '

Alison wasn't sure what she meant, but of one thing she was certain, she would not be visiting the general office at Beresfords . . . now or ever . . .

15

David had guessed they'd arrive around tea time . . . he had also found out on the grapevine such small towns always have, that they would be staying at the Golden Lion . . . he had made up his mind exactly what he was going to do and waited with ill concealed impatience . . . it was pure luck that he saw Alison leaving the pub without Susi for it made even easier what he had planned to do . . . for him life without Alison was not worth the living and he was going to risk everything on one last attempt to win her over . . .

He parked the Jag where she wouldn't see it on her return. Mrs.Barlow was making up the fire, he rubbed his hands at its warmth and smiled at her, they were old friends . . .

'I wondered if Mrs. Ross and Susi had arrived and if there was anything I could do, anything she was needing . . . '

The woman gave him a shrewd glance. It was pretty common knowledge that a close relationship of some sort had built up between him and Alison during the kidnapping — Mrs. Findlay sometimes came to the pub for a Guinness — she and Mrs. Barlow had known each other for years . . .

'Yes, they came before tea, but Mrs. Ross had to go out, she forgot to bring their toothbrushes. I promised to take young Susi up some hot milk . . . '

'I see,' he said slowly, 'do you think I might go up and see her? We are well acquainted, and we have a little unfinished business in the shape of a kind of serial story!'

She laughed, 'I'm sure Mrs. Ross wouldn't mind, and you can save my legs a journey by taking up the milk and biscuits . . . I was just going up to see the little maid when I'd finished the glasses . . . she may be feeling lonely in a strange room . . . '

He could see her through the half open door. She sat up in bed with Huggy beside her, reading a book, her head half turned from him, her profile so like her mother's that for a moment, caught off guard, he gave a sharp exclamation.

The child glanced up as he pushed the door open and went into the room. For a moment she looked surprised — then giving a squeal of delight, flung herself into his arms.

'Uncle David, Uncle David . . . ' she buried her face in his neck, her arms almost suffocating him as she clasped him tightly, and the sweet, warm smell of her filled his nostrils . . .

At last she released him as he gasped for breath, laughing and tickling her so that she squirmed and gurgled with delight . . . 'You've come to tell me more about Helpful Rabbit, I know you have, I told Huggy you would . . . ' Gently he tucked her back in bed but she wouldn't let his hand go and clung to him, Huggy once more forgotten as she begged him for the story, to tell her all Helpful Rabbit had been doing since last she heard about him . . .

Having seen him up the stairs, Mrs. Barlow went back into the kitchen to prepare the bar snacks, so Alison didn't see her and went straight up the narrow, twisting stairs, totally unaware that David was with Susi . . .

The door still stood ajar, but it wasn't till she reached the landing that she heard a man's voice coming from the bedroom . . . for a moment panic rose inside her . . . but as she heard the words, the tone . . . she realised whose voice it was and stood rooted to the spot, unable to move or speak . . . she hadn't expected this . . . not to see him alone . . . she had thought they would meet first in court surrounded by other people, officials, lawyers, police — and Mitch — not on her own in intimate confrontation like it had been before . . . and her heart couldn't tell her what to do . . . she pushed the hair back from her warm face . . .

As she listened she heard what David was saying. The name of Helpful Rabbit, Susi's little cries and exclamations of delight . . . she was unwilling to break the spell he was weaving . . . then the tone changed . . . no sounds now came from Susi as he said . . . 'poor Helpful Rabbit had never been so sad, his heart was quite broken, he was the most unhappy rabbit ever because Rebecca Rabbit, with whom he had fallen in love, had left him, gone to live in another burrow miles away . . . she didn't want to stay with him, to share his burrow at all . . . so the summer now meant nothing to him, he didn't even want to help the visitors on their way to the moor and beaches . . . he'd even lost his appetite for the juicy lettuces in the neighbours' gardens, even clover, which everyone knows is amongst a rabbit's favourite food . . . none of it tempted him and he got thinner and thinner and sadder and sadder, so he just lay in his burrow, his head on his paws, not even bothering to

clean himself or polish his white scut
. . . in fact he decided to sell his burrow
and go right away, live somewhere else
to try and forget her . . . '

His voice stopped. For a moment
there was a silence. Then Susi's voice
very quiet and subdued, on the edge of
tears, Alison could tell . . .

'But Uncle David, that isn't the end
is it? I mean why doesn't that silly
Rebecca come back to him? She must
know he loves her, and how happy
they'd be living in his burrow . . . why is
she so stupid? If I were her I'd marry
H.R. tomorrow, I think he's a lovely
Rabbit . . . even a bit like you Uncle
David . . . ' She gave a little sob,
making Alison feel near tears herself . . .

David spoke again now. 'Well you see
this Rebecca, she'd heard some other
spiteful rabbits chatting, gossiping, and
being rather a sensitive lady, she took it
to heart and ran off . . . but sometimes
rabbits, like people, don't know what's
best for them and it takes a third

person, someone outside the situation, like you or Huggy Bear for instance, to explain how foolish they're being . . . I think we shall have to work along those lines, see how things pan out . . . '

As Alison stood there in the quiet of the landing, the evening sun slanting through the window, motes of dust dancing in its golden rays, she realised exactly what the story meant . . . that David had simply been talking about himself, loosely disguised as his imaginary character . . .

Panic filled her again. She couldn't possibly face him at this moment, now with the fresh, wonderful knowledge that he did truly love her, that all her stupid fears had been ill founded . . . she looked round wildly for somewhere to hide and pulled open the door nearest to her . . . she had to have time to think, to adjust . . . she found it was a broom cupboard, and left the door a fraction open so she could hear and see . . . David said goodnight to Susi . . . then she felt him near her as he passed and even from that distance, her heart beat more quickly, so wildly she was sure he must hear it in the stillness of the passageway . . . but his footsteps receded down the stairs, she opened the cupboard door and went into the bedroom.

Susi was lying with Huggy clasped in her arms, her lashes bright with tears . . . She sat up and Alison drew her into her arms . . .

'What is it love? Were you lonely or frightened? You haven't drunk your milk . . . '

The child clung to her, hiding her face, still hiccuping with little sobbing sounds . . .

'It was Uncle David . . . didn't you see him?' Without waiting for an answer, she went on, 'It's H.R., he's so unhappy, he's not even eating, he may just pine away and die . . . all because that silly Rebecca won't come back and marry him . . . she doesn't realise how much he loves her you see . . . and he's not sure if she's in love with someone else . . . ' It all came tumbling out breathlessly . . . and for a moment Alison felt a stab of anger that David should have upset Susi, she was usually such a happy child, but she realised now there was more behind her tears and unhappiness than just the story — she had missed David, was as unsettled as Alison herself and the rather sad little tale had only emphasised this fact . . .

'After all, I've promised to marry Stevie when we're old enough, and I shan't go back on my promise . . . I think Rebecca's being ridiculous . . . ' she said to her mother with a touch of defiance . . .

'Look darling, we all make mistakes, grown ups as well as children and rabbits, and how do you know you'll still love Stevie after all that time?'

'I just know,' her small jaw set firmly now, a slight stubborness in her eyes as she looked at her mother . . .

Alison sighed. 'People change, times change . . . even love changes . . . ' as she spoke she heard a slight sound behind her and getting up from the bed, turned swiftly.

David stood in the doorway. For a moment neither of them moved as silently they looked at each other . . . all the longing spilled from his eyes . . . it seemed an eternity to her . . . was it too late or too soon to hope, to believe the story he had been telling Susi was really about himself. Could she rebuild a crazy dream that might come true? She was suddenly conscious of a kind of soaring feeling in her heart as at last he came towards her . . . and she heard Susi's sobs turned once more to chuckles of pure delight . . .

She went into the haven of his arms, he held her close to his heart as he might have a child, wholly protective, murmuring her name, words of love and comfort . . . with a sigh that was at last an abandonment of all doubt, of all fear, she leaned against him and they rocked together for a moment . . . Then Susi clasped her hands . . . 'Uncle

David, you've come back to tell me it's all right about H.R. haven't you —'

Releasing Alison for a moment he smiled and nodded at the child . . . then he said, 'Yes, it's going to be all right, Susi. H.R's lady love has come back to him . . . ' and in Alison's ear he murmured, 'I want to marry you . . . please . . . just as soon as possible, these weeks have been sheer hell without you . . . I want to look after you and Susi . . . ' he paused for a moment, and then held her away from him a little, his arms straight, his hands on her shoulders so that he looked down into her eyes . . . 'You can't deny you love me. I can see it in your eyes, whatever your lips may tell me . . . '

Too full of emotion for words, she nodded, her smile like spring sunshine after the warm rain of tears . . . gently he led her over to where Susi bounced up and down on the bed . . . and then the three of them sat there, while tears of joy ran down Alison's cheeks — tears of immeasurable relief because now everything was going to be all right . . . he drew her into his arms again, holding her safe and secure . . . and she thought perhaps for the first time in her whole life she had come home at last . . . and that was how it was going to be from now on . . . David — lover, husband, protector — and father for Susi . . . solid and dependable, always there . . . forever there . . . and like a small child, she dropped her head on his shoulder with a little sigh of perfect happiness and content . . .

We do hope that you have enjoyed reading this large print book.

Did you know that all of our titles are available for purchase?

We publish a wide range of high quality large print books including:
Romances, Mysteries, Classics
General Fiction
Non Fiction and Westerns

Special interest titles available in large print are:
The Little Oxford Dictionary
Music Book, Song Book
Hymn Book, Service Book

Also available from us courtesy of Oxford University Press:
Young Readers' Dictionary
(large print edition)
Young Readers' Thesaurus
(large print edition)

For further information or a free brochure, please contact us at:
Ulverscroft Large Print Books Ltd.,
The Green, Bradgate Road, Anstey,
Leicester, LE7 7FU, England.
Tel: (00 44) **0116 236 4325**
Fax: (00 44) **0116 234 0205**

THE FOOLISH HEART

Patricia Robins

Mary Bradbourne's aunt brought her up after her parents died. When she was ten, her aunt had a son, Jackie, who was left with a mental disability as the result of an accident. Unselfish and affectionate, Mary dedicated her life to caring for him. But when she meets Dr. Paul Deal and falls in love with him she faces a dilemma. How will she be able to care for her cousin, when she knows she must follow her heart?